THE MURDER OF VINCENT van GOGH

The Murder of Vincent van Gogh

ISBN 978-0-578-00312-2
www.writeshott.com

"But there is a God in heaven that revealeth secrets…and he that revealeth secrets
maketh known to thee what shall come to pass."
Daniel 2:28-29, KJV

It is a little known fact that
Vincent van Gogh was a preacher.

DISCLAIMER

This is a story about Vincent van Gogh, but it is not a historical biography. What you will read is a tribute to Vincent van Gogh: a book that invents characters and situations that reach beyond reality to express what might have been Vincent van Gogh's inner experience on his unique life-journey.

Unlike conventional biography, this story takes a bold step of merging reality and fantasy. It is a work that deals with things totally invented, during a period of time in which little is known.

For historians, there were periods of time when Vincent van Gogh did not write to his brother (perhaps not to anyone, unless future letters emerge) and there were times when he simply disappeared (going on long, unaccompanied walks). Times of disappearance are one of the heart chambers of the mystery genre.

So this story tries to tell what happened during those disappearances but also during the times when he disappeared mentally and spiritually. It is a free adaptation based on immersion into the writings of Vincent van Gogh that has attempted to channel a great artist's voice both in style and craft.

This story, The Murder of Vincent van Gogh, had one goal: tell what *could* have been.

Was Vincent van Gogh murdered? That question can only be answered with logical supposition: when it is impossible to prove the truth (or untruth) of a thing then truth matters little. Therefore, what is known as the truth could be a lie and, contrary-wise, what is believed a lie may prove Truth.

There is one incontrovertible fact, Vincent van Gogh (the famous and infamous 19th century painter) was shot and died.

Let us begin this tale where all good murders begin: a body. Not Vincent van Gogh's, but a woman's.

The Year: 1879.

The place: Le Chat Noir...

"Who is that woman?" Theo asked his friend Andres.

"I don't know. I'd bet she's Dutch."

"But of course. Do you know anyone at her table?"

"I've seen that young man," Andres pointed to a nicely dressed blonde man, "At the Dutch Club."

"Funny. I haven't."

"I believe he's…an actor."

Theo hit his friend's shoulder, "As if that would make any difference to me. I must find out more about her."

Andres looked at the woman more intently then turned to Theo, "May I ask why?"

"Because, dear Bonger, she is the epitome of Dutch beauty!"

Andres emptied his cloudy-green down his throat and waived to a waitress {who'd caught his eye} that he should receive another absinthe.

"If you say so, my friend," Andres laughed, "If you say so."
***

Meanwhile, Theo's brother—Vincent—was amidst a great human suffering: the mines of the Borinage.
    The Borinage lay south of Vincent's homeland,

[Holland]
and still south in its own country

    —Belgium—

as if it were disaffected kin, pushed out to the very edge of association and there it remained,
along
        the
                Mons river,
set across from

        |away from|

separated from its neighbor-land: France.

    One brother|to each side.

    That their lives there, each respectively, would be as disparate should not prove difficult to understand.

One brother consumed by being a Christian...
the other, by being a man.
***

In Paris:

"Do you have a table for us, Salis?" Theo, discretely, palmed the man his dues.

"But of course, Messr van Gogh, right over here."

The formality was all play: each person played his or her part. Melodrama was the forum allotted Le Chat.

However there was a prerequisite in landing such roles, *money*. So it (money) became the staging ground upon which the tables were set (for drinks to be laid upon). It (*it*) also, depending on the size of its mons determined, which tables sat next to which—so like a grand coliseum,

                    neatly ordered strata

            in order that those with *it*

      could easily be witness (and bear witness against):

      to those with and without (it). Theo van Gogh sat

      at a very good table.

A week had passed since Theo had seen his Dutch Beauty. He waited, anxiously, for his friend Andres to arrive from his job, [clerking], however it was still early. Outside, the Boulevard Rochechouart still teamed with legitimate trade. It would not be until after the light of each day faded that the trades exchanged: grains for girls (and many other things, then, went bump in the night).

It *was* early.

Being a proper proprietor, Messr Sallis knew that there was nothing more dangerous to his trade than a man drinking alone so, in spite of the fact that he did not entirely enjoy Theo's company (nor any of the Dutch—being a true-blooded Frenchman), he assumed his role's character and, with great attempt to make his client feel welcome (for welcomed patrons patronized well), he sat at Theo's table. For a bit...he sipped a dark red wine. Theo had begun his absinthe.

Sallis watched his waiters and waitresses scammering. Women tied back bits of hair. Men slicked down corners of moustaches. All arrayed in a plethora of garb: green berets, gold soldier's braids hung about plump juicy {plum breasts} and an Academician's gown |with highest laurels~cords tied tight round the waist with just such a golden braid| in the fashion of a toga on a girl from Scandinavia (she was a club favorite).

Whatever one's favorite issue, topic or scandal: it could be found at Le Chat Noir. In fact, as Salis sat at Theo's table, in walked a friar: an actor who'd tried desperately to get a role but settled for Sallis' waiter's wage in exchange for shaving a small plate atop his head. With humility, he served his customers what they desired (both in front of and behind the stage).
Salis, himself, laughed at this one: "He might just make it."
"Oh? Make it where?" Theo asked.
"The stage."
"Here?"
"Anywhere. Here, I guess."
"Yes, but Salis. Your crowd can get a little critical."
Salis laughed, slapping his thigh, "That's putting it mildly kid. Say. Where's your friend?"
"Still working I think."
"He better watch out. That stuff will kill you."
        Theo looked at his greenish-white.
        Salis stood up, "I meant work, kid."
        Just then Theo saw Andres at the bar, ordering. He could hardly stand the waiting. Andres had agreed that, during the week, he'd be on a secret mission: engage the Dutch man he'd recognized at the table (that night) and, through wiles and means, discover the identity of the mysterious Dutch Beauty. As soon as Andres' trousers touched the seat's seat Theo began: "Tell me, Bonger, did you find out anything?"
"Easy, Theo. Easy. All in good time."
        Andres sipped his absinthe. Savoring his friend's angst.
"Oh come now Andres. No fair!"
"Yes. Dear Theo. Yes. I found out about your Dutch Beauty."
        Theo bobbed his head up and down, silently begging his friend to divulge, when suddenly Andres pointed to the stage.
        It was unbelievable! There she was, dressed as a common whore, tapping her foot in accompaniment with a brash accordionist, swishing a cheaply-laced skirt over her head, and showing her knickers, stockings, garters and black fish-netted.
***

Fire-damp explosions were what Vincent knew hell would be. An eternity of firedamp—an eternity of ironic juxtaposition between what should prove balance,

{fire|damp}

but what is (in fact) death. The Borinage.

He'd been in the Borinage but shortly when the first came. 300 bodies. Men, women, young men, young women, and children (boys/girls): the blasts were non-discriminant. They killed with the mercy of equality.

But the physically dead worried Vincent less than the barely-living. The corpses-to-be that stretched across the spring-damp mud—the sludge of—the mine's mouth and teethy-gums. It was those people, whose last few moments ticked quickly down, that haunted Vincent. For it was those souls Vincent's soul tormented itself with questioning: were they saved?

This desperation made him scamper, like a ravenous mouse, chittering into the eldest ears first (for he knew that God spared the innocence of children): "Have you accepted Christ as your living Saviour?"

If they acquiesced, he said a quick blessing for them and ran—like Mustang—to the next elder body. If they denied, he had no choice; he had to try: "Jesus Christ died on the cross for you, Brother (or Sister) because he loves you. You are going to meet your Maker. Please accept Christ and know eternal Salvation!"

This was the last chance the dying was given. They either did—or died. And many died that day. But there was one: a woman—whose small son (aged 8 or thereabouts) clung to his mother's bloody body—that smiled a smile so peaceful and serene. She even held her hand up to Vincent's face, touching his red, stubblehaired skin, "Bless you, my son," she said…and died.

The little boy hugged her, crying. Vincent cried, as sincere as the boy in him would tear, but physically took the boy from his mother…holding him tight, though the child squirmed mercilessly to escape. His efforts to comfort the boy

were frustrated by the child's sorrow, which proved stronger than muscle, and the boy escaped back to his dead mother's body. The cries of more dying penetrated that scene: a scene like none ever painted in all the paintings Vincent had ever seen: the scarlet crimson and cobalt black bore down hard upon him until an old man's panting breath managed to reach through: "Help me!" The old man managed.
"Have you accepted…"

The old man must have heard Vincent speaking to those around him, "Yes. Bless me, Father."
"But I'm not…"
"Bless me, Father."
"God bless you and keep you now and…"

The man's eyes superimposed: devoid of life.
"…forever. Amen."

Vincent closed the lids. It was a formality—a fleshly coffin.

The boy came to him. Vincent held out his arms. The child ran into them.
"Father. Help my Mommy!"

His heart broke then, for the man in him. And he quietly prayed, "God help me! I know not what to do!" Then he heard himself saying to the boy, "Your Mommy doesn't need my help. She's has the help of the greatest Father in all of the world—in all the Universe—and she's with him right now. With him in Heaven and she'll be there, surrounded with gold and pearls and never be hungry again—or in pain."

The boy hugged Vincent, crying onto his shoulder, "But I want my Mommy now! Can I go to Heaven to see her?"
"She'll always be with you, if you believe in Jesus."

The boy looked Vincent straight in the eye. "Then I believe, Father."

He didn't have the heart to tell him he wasn't a Father. That he was the lowest of the low, according to the Institution of religion (of which his own father belonged)—for he was simply an evangelical. Unpaid even. He did not merit the title, "Father."

He had not passed Greek or Latin,
had not formally studied at Seminary—
he simply read,
faithfully read,
fanatically read,
with his whole-heart read the Bible and pledged his life to do
God's will.
***

At Le Chat:

"My God, Andres, look at her!"
"Yes, Theo. She's the most beautiful girl *I've* ever seen;" the
tone of his drone implied that the opposite was true.
"And how she moves! I tell you, Bonger. I must meet her!"
    Andres sipped his drink. A fine red-headed waitress
dressed in folk had given him a ;wink—or he was pretty sure
she had—so when she came to ask if he'd like another drink he
felt license to touch the silk of her thigh, to which she replied,
"I'll meet you."
    That was the codex (I'll meet you), the "password" and it
was necessary because not all of the waitresses (or waiters)
would settle on prices (—later—in the dark of rooms
somewhere in Montmartre). But most would, only the few
some simply performed: the other rest completely sold flesh.
    Codes aside, the red-headed girl's 'I'll meet you' put
Andres in a fine mood. He liked the freedom of whores. He'd
been raised, much like Theo, to be morally upstanding and
rigidly proper (though devilishly human). Paris was the very
breath he needed to live—having left his family in Amsterdam.
The culture, the politics, the drugs and women—the art: in
Paris—any and every excuse to indulge his flesh…and good
food.
    None of this hedonism reached Theo at that moment, for
he was smitten (and was absolutely sure that the lips of his
Dutch Beauty would never express, "I'll meet you." In fact,
when Andres as much as suggested so, Theo cuffed his
friend's ear and yelled, "Unthinkable!").
    Theo learned, that night, that he'd been correct: his utter
belief in her honor, vindicated. His Dutch Beauty's denial
proved that fact. However, she did eventually accept Theo's
money, in exchange for: "talking only."
***

13

The Saturday after the explosion Vincent could not sleep. He could not eat, nor even think, clearly. What could he possibly say to all those poor people—from where he stood—upon a great responsibility: the pulpit—that would honor God, that would elevate God...that would give the gift of knowing the love of God to a people suffering so greatly?

He grasped at sermons. He read what he'd written before, about topics, understandings, and interpreting the Scriptures, but felt the impotence of his own words.

Nothing stirred him.

He prayed for the Holy Spirit to guide him, to use him in order to help His people.

Yet he felt useless. Like that day—outside the mine.

He fell to his knees and repeatedly thrust his head against his Bible, which rested upon his bed. His ears heard: "thud" "thud" "thud" as the book thrust itself into the mattress. "Dear God," he cried out, "Help me. What am I to say?"

Then he prayed in that quiet way, in an attitude of supplication and humility. And then he opened the Word of God: "Mathew," he heard in that sacred place—that place of prayer where he knew he knelt before the throne...at the foot of God.

The pages of the Bible fluttered—though scarcely a breeze penetrated the musty air of his room—as if the book's edge danced with invisible fingers—there, before his eyes, he saw with the clarity of a hawk:

Mathew 15...17...21.

"And Jesus departed from thence, and came nigh unto the sea of Galilee; and went up into the mountain, and sat down there. And great **multitudes** came unto him, having with them those that were lame, blind, dumb, **maimed**, and many others, and cast them down at Jesus' feet; and he healed them: insomuch that the multitude wondered, when they saw the dumb to speak, **the maimed to be whole,** the lame to walk, and the blind to see: **and they glorified the God of Israel**. Mt 15:29-31"

"And when they were come to the **multitude**, there came to him a certain man, kneeling down to him, and saying, Lord, have mercy on my son: for he is a lunatick, and sore vexed: for ofttimes he falleth into the fire, and oft into the water. And I brought him to thy disciples, and they could not cure him. Then Jesus answered and said, O faithless and perverse generation, how long shall I be with you? bring him hither to me. And Jesus rebuked the devil; and he departed out of him: and the child was cured from that very hour. Then came the disciples to Jesus apart, and said, Why could not we cast him out? And Jesus said unto them, Because of your unbelief; for verily I say unto you, **If ye have faith** as a grain of mustard seed, ye shall say unto this **mountain, Remove** hence to yonder place; and it shall remove; and nothing shall be impossible unto you. Howbeit this kind goeth not out but by **prayer and fasting**. Mt 17: 14-21"

"And the **multitude** said, This is Jesus the prophet of Nazareth of Galilee. And Jesus went into the temple of God, and cast out all them that sold and bought in the temple, and overthrew the tables of the money-changers, and the seats of them that sold doves, and said unto them, It is written, **My house shall be called the house of prayer; but ye have made it a den of thieves.** And the blind and the lame came to him in the temple; and he healed them. And when the chief priests and scribes saw the wonderful things that he did, and the **children crying in the temple, and saying, Hosanna to the Son of David;** they were sore displeased. And said unto him, Hearest thou what these say? **And Jesus saith unto them, Yea; have ye never read, Out of the mouth of babes and sucklings thou hast perfected praise**? And he left them, and went out of the city into Bethany; and he lodged there.

Now in the morning as he returned into the city, **he hungered.** And when he saw a fig tree in the way, **he came to it, and found nothing thereon, but leaves only, and said unto it, Let no fruit grow on thee henceforward fore ever. And presently the fig tree withered away.** And when the disciples saw it, they marveled, saying, How soon is the fig tree withered away! Jesus answered and said unto them, Verily I say unto you, **If ye have faith,** and doubt not, ye shall not only do this which is done to the fig tree, but also if ye shall say unto this **mountain, Be thou removed**, and be thou cast into the sea; it shall be done. **And all things, whatsoever ye shall ask in prayer, believing, ye shall receive.** Mt 21: 11-22"

Then Vincent knew what had to be said and he praised God for allowing him to be an instrument of guidance and comfort for His suffering people.

Still, that Sunday morning, having fasted (consuming nothing but bread and water since the accident)—he felt himself weak and nervous, scared to death that what might issue from his mouth would prove…ineffective.

"Brothers and Sisters, many of you are suffering today. It has been a time of great sorrow, a time of loss and pain. For those surviving the accident, those injured and maimed, there is ongoing anxiety for your families and yourselves. But you must remember that we are to praise God in _**all**_ things. Even in

16

bad things, for that is where faith is. And when we join together, in multitudes such as this, and praise God then He promises us that, through His power, even mountains can be moved into the sea or moved from here to there," Vincent pointed from one side of the room to the other.

"Yet I know how very hard it is to hear the cries of the suffering, especially the children, and wonder how God can allow such pain—can this be God's will for us?

"Children," Jesus says himself, "mouth perfect praise." This praising of God then, is exactly what we ***must*** do...for...the children. So that they call out, "Hosanna!" and are saved by the beautiful grace of God. Because Christ also cautions us that when he hungers for the fruits of us, perhaps meaning—our children—and when we (as the tree bearing those fruits) have not produced fruit for Christ...then the tree is then barren forevermore...and it withers away...and dies.

Christ loves you. He loves your children. He hears your sufferings and He suffers with you, not separate from you. When you cry...he cries. But through your faith, He can heal your wounds—he can make you whole where you are lame— he can give you salvation where ***all*** of His children are united forever—in Heaven.

So that even now, in this time of great despair, He gives the greatest opportunity to praise Him. To give to Him what He hungers for: your love, your faith...your trust."

"John Bunyan wrote, "The Pilgrim's Progress." It is a very good book and for any who'd like to hear it I'd be happy to read for you. But essentially it says that our life is a Pilgrim's Progress.

When I envision the place Bunyan speaks of I see a very beautiful picture: a landscape at evening. In the distance, on the right-hand side, are rows of hills that appear blue in the evening mist. Above those hills there is a splendorous sunset with gray clouds lined with silver and gold and purple. The land itself is plain, or perhaps is a heath, covered with grass and yellow, Autumnal leaves. Through the landscape a road winds and on this road travels a pilgrim. He is carrying a staff and has been walking a very long time. He is tired and the road he is traveling on leads up, up, up towards a tall mountain, which is far away. He can barely see the mountaintop but notices a city is there, whereon the setting sun casts a glory.

It seems an overwhelming journey, yet on the road he meets a woman—a figure in black—that makes him think of St. Paul's reminder that in sorrow one must rejoice. That woman is an angel of God. God sent her to the pilgrim in that very moment, when he was looking up towards that mountaintop, that city of light, which seemed so very far away and feeling, perhaps as you might now—despair—in order that the angel could guide the pilgrim on his journey.

So the weary pilgrim asks, "Does the road go uphill then...*all* the way?" To which the angel replies, "Yes. To the very end."

And the pilgrim asks again, "And will the journey take all day long?"

And the angel answers, "From morn till night, my friend." So the pilgrim continues on, sorrowful—because he is so far from the mountain city—but rejoicing because he knows that the city, with all its resplendent evening glow, is waiting—with great anticipation—for his assured arrival."

"Brother and Sisters you must now be brave and ***know*** that God loves you! He is waiting for you. He understands that this road—this life—is very, very hard but He promises you that He will not leave you alone in your times of struggle, of weariness—and when you need Him all you have to do is pray,
have faith,
and love him with all your hearts. Amen."

Thus ended Vincent's sermon.

Afterwards, the miners shook his hand as they left to return to their hard lives.

A little boy, the 8-year old boy whose mother had died, came up to Vincent, pulled at his sleeve and asked, "Father, is that city in your story where Mommy is?"

Vincent knelt down to the boy's level. How could he put it? Bunyan's story was far more complicated than that.
"What's your name?" Vincent asked.
"Tommy."
"Well, Tommy. Do you work in the mine yet?"

"No. Not yet. I think soon. Grandma says. Since Mommy died."

"Well, I'll come see you tomorrow and I'll tell you more of the story okay?"

"Oh yes, Father!"

Vincent stood up, "But you mustn't call me Father anymore. You must call me Vincent."

"Okay. See you tomorrow."

The little boy grabbed his grandmother's hand. Vincent saw that the woman couldn't have been more than thirty years old—and that, even, was probably older than she was...for living mining lives aged people beyond God-given years. And those who managed to live past thirty rarely looked younger than those grayed with the grace of natural long-aging.
***

Chapter: The First Betrayal

Theo van Gogh was not hard to look at. He was blonde-ish. He had rather fine features (albeit a relatively fragile frame which, perhaps, impressed upon others more lastingly than any of his other physical aspects) yet carried himself with a combustible air of humility/arrogance. These characteristics (physical and emotional) being both equally balanced meant women, in general, found him near-irresistible (particularly those at Le Chat Noir where some had even given him the pet name "little brother" because he'd managed to endear himself to their hearts…or was, which may have been more likely the case, simply so frequently present at Le Chat that it was as if he were part of their 'family').

So when Salis approached his newest entertainer (a young Dutch girl who went by the name of See) he assured her that Theo van Gogh was a gentleman, a charming man and—most importantly—a good (meaning: wealthy) customer.

See, however, was not easily swayed. She'd come from a middleclass family (or at least it had been. Her father was in the cotton business, which fluctuated like waves on the sea. And at that particular time—the tide was out which was why See had come to Paris looking for work. She had not told her parents that she'd secretly always wanted to perform on stage—just as she'd failed to tell them where her place of employment was; they'd been led to believe—by See—that she was working as a washerwoman).

See, however, made sure Salis understood that she was most definitely NOT a whore.
"Come, come," Salis condemned, "Surely if Messr. van Gogh wanted a whore he'd have chosen a much prettier one than you!" Still, it cost Salis more than what he'd wanted to pay for See to agree to spend an evening with the man. But Salis knew how to treat his best customers—he knew how to keep them coming back…again and again and again.

Theo waited in the audience for See to finish. It was close to midnight before the "Dutch Beauty" had changed and was ready to go. When Theo approached her she looked at him as a cattlebuyer looks at potential stock. She was not impressed. For unlike many of the women at Le Chat Noir, she'd grown up around respectable men and this young man's "mixture" of personality (or persona) struck inferior or insincere—she could not, immediately, determine which.

"Hello." Theo said, smiling. "I'm Theo van Gogh."

"I know who you are," replied See.

"And Salis made the appropriate arrangements with you?"

"That is correct."

He could hardly believe his ears. She was a true beauty. Her manner. Her looks. He was smitten, besotted, and dumbstruck: he could not help himself—he touched her arm. She reeled from him as if his skin pored acid.

"I don't know what you think our "agreement" is but I assure you, Sir, it does NOT involve you making inappropriate gestures!"

"I'm very sorry. I meant no offence…it's just that I…"

"I will not tolerate you treating me as you might assume that you can. I am not *that* type of woman."

"I know that. I could never think *that!*"

See wanted to leave him standing there. Nothing about him appealed to her…but Salis had paid her to spend that one evening. One evening only. And what he'd paid for her to spend the next 8 hours of her life with this small, sickly-looking man was more than what she'd make on the stage in three weeks. So she did what any levelheaded woman does: she slapped his face. Hard.

They walked out of Le Chat Noir. The middlenight's darkness hid the red handmark she'd left on his left cheek.

***

After his sermon, Vincent went to his room. He'd already moved from the peddler's house to the baker's house
(because it was closer to the mine...and nearer the miners)
but something about the peddler's/baker's places struck a disharmonizing chord. They were nice: clean, neat, large rooms and the food was good—it was all wrong. Why? Ever since he'd arrived at the Borinage mines he'd been asking himself the "why" for his discomfort. After his sermon, the answer struck in the shapes of Mathew's words...

"**If ye have faith** as a grain of mustard seed, ye shall say unto this **mountain, Remove** hence to yonder place; and it shall remove; and nothing shall be impossible unto you. Howbeit this kind goeth not out but by **prayer and fasting**."

He knew what he had to do. He immediately went to the baker's wife and informed her he'd be leaving. When she asked why he wanted to change accommodations, he simply said that it was not right for him to live in such luxury while the miners lived with very much less. That if he wanted to be a good minister to them, he needed to live as they lived.

Even though she pled with him to stay (as she—and her husband—had become used to the income they'd been receiving from Vincent's father) he refused. This was not well-received and the baker's wife, after having watched Vincent pack his things and head towards the miner's houses, set about straight away in drafting a letter to Vincent's father explaining that his son had, in fact, altogether, lost his senses.
***

To his pleasurable surprise Theo discovered, during his walking of his Dutch Beauty to her home, that they lived quite near to each other (and to Le Chat). However, this did not afford him the time he'd planned (for getting to know her better) but he still made what attempt he could by asking her questions that she, dutifully, answered.

For example:

"What is your name?"

"See."

"That's an unusual name. You are Dutch?"

"Yes."

"And See is your name?"

"Yes. See."

"Is it a nickname?"

"Yes."

"For what?"

"Classina."

And thusly the conversation went on: tediously, painstakingly—just as a gardener working to eradicate crabgrass from a lawn. See thanked God the reach of time between Le Chat and her apartment's sanctuary was short.

"May I come in?" Theo asked.

See thought. She shared the one-room apartment with three other stagegirls.

All four took turns sleeping in the one small bed and, at that time of night, it would have been nearly guaranteed that at least one would be there—if not all—depending on when Salis had them performing (or if they were 'offstage.' For See's three roommates were the kinds of girls that used the password, "I'll meet you,"…often).

But Salis had paid her to speak with Theo for the 'night' and the night was still, relatively, young. So, to Theo's pleasant surprise, See asked if they could go to his place to 'visit' instead. Which was, literally, around the corner…and across the street.

During the crossing, See took a good look at the young man by her side. He was skinny and slight. He made her think of the skeletons people painted for All Soul's Eve. And his face was pointed, making his blue eyes seem deeper—like shallow pools found underground…in caves.

They climbed a narrow staircase, walked down a long hall, and—through a scratched and worn old door—entered into quite a remarkable room. It was a space that greatly impressed the young See. There was an expensive settee, an expensive dining table with matching sideboard and chairs, a china cupboard filled (and with expensive crystal) and a bar stocked with a plethora of colored and shaded liquors. The room conveyed wealth. See knew what wealth looked like.

"You like it?" Theo asked, waving his hand in a semi-circle to encompass the eye's view of his room.

See looked at the corner. There stood a bed, separated from the rest of the area by screens displaying Japanese scenes. She pointed to them, "I've never seen anything like that before. Where did you get them?"

"A friend of mine, an artist, did those for me. You might know him, Lautrec?"

"No."

"Yes, that's right, I forget that you're new at Le Chat. Well, you will know Lautrec. He's always there."

Theo went to the bar. "May I offer you a drink?"

"No thank you."

"You sure?"

"Yes. And you know that all we're going to be doing is talking."

"I'm not trying to get you drunk and take advantage of you if that's what you're implying."

"I'll leave 'implication' up to you. I just want to make sure that we're both clear on that matter."

"Crystal. Now would you like a drink?"

See sighed. She had more hours to spend with him and not a thought as to what on earth they'd talk about. Besides, one drink couldn't hurt. "Okay. Scotch."

"With water?"

"No."

Theo smiled and thought, "My Beauty."

One led to two and two to three and from there they became exponential until both had dried up a significant portion of Theo's bar—until somewhere, off in the distance, a rooster crowed.

Looking out of Theo's window See watched a windmill twisting itself around an invisible wind. Theo had long-fallen asleep from drink. He snored, sprawled atop his settee.

See tiptoed across the floor, cracked the squeaky old door—which caused Theo to shift his body's weight—and slunk back to her apartment, weavingly drunk, where she collapsed on the floor and slept a hard good three hours before one of her roommates violently shook her awake: it was nearly time for her to go onstage.
***

Vincent waited just outside the 'village' where the miners lived (though the villagers of the main village effectively claimed the miner's houses 'not village' but an 'enclave'—separate from their wealthy houses and wealthy shops). He watched as,
door-by-door,
they filed out
into almost neat
lines heading towards
the mine's mouthgape
which, literally—with its grimacing lips—
faced each homeplace and exhaled its pungent breath
into every waking nostril.

Their clothes, even when washed clean, were perpetually soiled gray
from coaldust embedded deep within the fiber's knit—
woven, even still, deep within each one of the men and women and children whose spittle shimmered oily black when they hacked themselves out in coughing
fits at the end of their daily shifts.

Vincent knocked on the door to little Tommy's house. Tommy's grandmother opened it. She'd lived with Tommy ever since the mine had made her a widow (a decade ago). She never thought she'd be playing mother again—but welcomed the warmth of snuggling, as Tommy, in particular, mourned his mother's fate awfully hard.

The house was just like every other miners' wooden shack.
Littlelight
[luminosity was luxurious]—
{only wealthy could afford that which windows cost}:
|heat|

and moss thatched roofs meant, in the darkness, there was never enough coal to keep them warm   in the fall, winter or spring. For even though spring could be clement—it was as often as not:
|cold|.

Tommy's grandmother kept a frayed shawl about her shoulders. She offered Vincent the last gulps of coffee (a sacrifice of the only coffee she'd get herself that day). She was secretly thankful to God when he refused, saying, "I came here today because Tommy wanted to know more about a book called Pilgrim's Progress."

"The one you preached?" His grandmother asked.

"Yes. Well sort of. I didn't exactly use the story as it is…just sort of my own feelings about it."

He could see an expression of confusion cross the old woman's face. "You see, the one I preached was sort of, well, condensed…but there's more…and look…" Vincent pulled from his bag a few sketches he'd made the night before.

"…I thought maybe if there were pictures then the story might be more interesting."

"Read it, Father. Read it!" Tommy shouted, as he ran into the room, having just finished picking dandelions for their lunch.

Vincent held up the first sketch. It was of a man walking with his head down because he was carrying a load upon his back.

"You see," Vincent said, noticing now that not only was the little boy entranced but his grandmother too, "this man's carrying something very heavy. Like the coal carriers."

Both the old woman and the boy smiled. They both understood what that meant.

"And the burden upon him is wearing him down."

The grandmother, suddenly, looked very sad.

"What is it?"

She was crying a little.

"My Tom, Tommy's grandpa, he wore himself plum out up there at that mine. That picture there makes me think of him."

And for a moment Vincent felt—a strange mixture within him. On one hand: sorrow for the woman's suffering…yet on the other…a sort of excitement…that his own hand could create such feeling in her. This latter sensation, however, quickly morphed into guilt over how he could derive any pleasure, whatsoever, from another's misfortune and so he quickly returned to the story.

"This man's name is Christian and he lives in a city named Destruction."

Then Vincent put forward his next drawing. The grandmother and the boy were both eager to see what came next. It was the man leaving his wife and children behind. This time it was Tommy who cried, pulling himself into his grandmother's side. The grandmother frowned at Vincent: (she did not like it when Tommy fell to hurting).

"I know this is hard for you Tommy," Vincent tried to comfort the boy, "But you see, Christian had to leave his family."

Tommy sniffled, "But why?"

"Well, because God had made the burden on his back so heavy that he couldn't stand it. That's when God came into his heart, and through the Bible, Christian learned that he needed to walk on the path God had set before him—the path to salvation. But when he told his wife about what he'd learned about God—and his call to follow God—she wouldn't go with him."

"But what about his kids?" the grandmother asked.

"She wouldn't let them go either."

"That's terrible!"

"Indeed, it is. But Christian kept to his decision and began walking away from everything that he loved in the world—just to follow God. And before you know it," Vincent said, pulling another picture out and showing it to the woman and boy, "along came…"

They both pealed with laughter. On the same page there were two figures: one looked like a half-mule/half-human and the other looked like a man with a blob of bread dough for his head.

"…Obstinate and Pliable."

Vincent told the story up to the point where Obstinate told Christian that he would lose all his friends, his family and his home if he continued to behave the way he was. It was the same point, in the story, where Pliable (who, at first, had encouraged Christian when Christian had doubted) gave up the path and ran back home—after having freed himself from the Slough of Despond.

Vincent did show them one more drawing. "This," Vincent said, "is Evangelist."

The man in the drawing expressed nothing short of peace and serenity (a near-Christ image in ink). The grandmother's and Tommy's faces seemed to lift just from seeing it. That was when Vincent rose to leave.

Tommy cried, "But aren't you going to tell us about Evangelist?"

"Next time, Tommy."

"Tomorrow!"

"Yes," the grandmother insisted, "Tomorrow. And you'll have coffee, by God. You'll have coffee!"

But before Vincent left he handed Tommy the drawing of Evangelist.

"I'll need that one for tomorrow's story. So don't loose it okay?"

He watched the boy's spirit rise for they both understood—his keeping of the picture was an unspoken guarantee of his return—such guarantees were hard-found around the mines...in the Borinage.

***

When Theo awoke he looked around for See but she was gone. He quickly washed, shaved and dressed. As usual, he was never late for work. He was the near-idyllic worker. Even though he'd only been working at the Paris branch of Goupil & Co. just over two months, he had come highly recommended (by his Uncle Cent, who had been one of the three original shareholders of Goupil & Co and who had only, just the year prior, cashed in his share of the company thereby making Theo's Uncle Cent a very rich man).

And money was the very thing Goupil respected. For the act of selling art was as if it were a distinct lifeform that breathed in singular atmospheric element: money, in order to breathe out: art.

And Goupil's, as a company, catered entirely to feeding the appetites of those who could pay, dearly, to consume (their central hall was long and tall and well-lit in order to give the sensation that one was at the Louvre or viewing works from the official Salon. All was served to sweeten and wet their client's appetites for "moral order" in the guise of gaiety and 'winners').

It was true that Theo had spent years, as an art dealer, at Goupil's Hague branch yet, in spite of his prior experience or his familial connections or the fact that he always looked outwardly chic (for Theo dressed in the finest suits, shirts and shoes available in Paris) there was something lacking in his ability to hardsell or, for that matter, to sell much at all.

It was, in fact, Paris itself that had brought Theo at odds with his employer's needs to feed the rich. It was, more specifically, Le Chat Noir—and Theo's associations with the Le Chat Noir artists

    (who were all too aware of his occupation as an art
    dealer and bombarded him with their hopes of becoming
    famous artists, if only the right dealer would represent
    them—the dealer with vision, strength and foresight)
had begun to infuse the young Dutch man's spirit with colors and unconventionality—all things the rich Bourgeois found distasteful...therefore precluded their appetite for buying art (of any kind).

And Theo sensed this too. For when he, as passionately and emphatically as he could, showed them the art of the 'real' artists—the Le Chat artists—he felt them squirm. Some would even ask, ever so politely, to see a certain piece or other that they'd heard of (at the Salon) and he would, then, adequately dawn his conventional charm and…sell, softly.

The art—the real art…the Le Chat art—never outsold tradition, not even the best of them. But he would console himself, after taking his commission, thinking, "If only they could see—lift from their eyes those veils of prejudice and conservatism—and really see what (fully) alive artists are doing (instead long dead ones) then they would understand art. Then they would buy."

This became foremost in his thought—that…and See.

***

The next day Vincent, again, waited for the miners to go to work but this time Tommy was already waiting for him outside his front door, in the chilled mist of early morning—and with him were three other children: two boys and a girl.

When Vincent approached, Tommy beamed and pointed to the boy closest to him: "This here's Jake. That there's Mark. And she's Mark's little sister—Marie." He pulled Vincent's coat sleeve to get him to bend down to his level and whispered in his ear, "She's a yucky girl but Mark said his Mom said he couldn't come without her."
"Oh," Vincent replied, "I see."

The girl, not more than two or three years old, grabbed (and held tight to) her older brother's hand. Vincent noticed how small they seemed—and how hollowly large her eyes were.
"So," Vincent said, looking back and forth over the four children, "I suppose you're here to hear a story?"
"Oh yes Father! Yes!" cried out the little girl, in a voice much bigger than she was.
"Well then, let's go inside out of the cold."

Inside, Tommy's grandmother had been waiting for the very moment Vincent came through the threshold just so that the last cup of coffee would be as hot as possible. "Here you go Father," the old woman beamed and sat down in an as-excited manner as the children.
"Thank you very much." He sipped, burning his tongue, but didn't dare show the pain for he knew all that the old woman had sacrificed to make things just so—coffee...and extra coal.
"Okay Tommy," Vincent began, "Do you have the picture I gave you of Evangelist?"
"Sure do!" he said, jumping up and shoving it—gently, however—into Vincent's hands.
"Very good. So it all began with Christian and his very heavy burden."
The little girl said, "What's a burthen?"
Tommy scoffed, "Like what your daddy does at the mine, stupid!"
"Now Tommy," Vincent reprimanded, "If you can't say something nice to Marie then you mustn't say anything at all.

Remember, God loves her just as much as He loves you—and me—and your mother."

This did not set well with Tommy. His dead mother just had to be more loved than that icky Marie. But Vincent sat, silent. And somehow Tommy knew that if he didn't say that he agreed—there'd be no more story.

"Okay, Father." Tommy mumbled.

"Very good. Now I'll begin."

But as soon as Vincent leaned over to pull his drawings from his bag Tommy whispered to Jake, "But my mom was never so stinky as she is." Jake giggled. Vincent, who'd heard, ignored it. After all, kids could only be expected to obey—most times.

***

It just so happened that on that day a very wealthy woman, and her chaperone, entered Goupil's and when Theo approached her she made no allusion to browsing or shopping—she was intent on purchase. This was music to Theo's, still hungover, ears for it had been a week since his last sale. No sales meant no commission, which meant the lifestyle he'd quickly accustomed himself to was rapidly running the young man to ruin.

"Madame," said Theo, bowing and kissing her gloved hand. "And Madame," he said to her escort, repeating the same genuflection (minus the hand-kissing).

"This," said the escort, "is Miss Bonger. I believe you know her brother, Messr Andres?"

"Yes, quite well."

Theo was taken aback; he'd heard Andres speak of his little sister but it was always with such disdain—claiming her calculative, cold and rather plain. But Theo found the woman in front of him direct, driven—albeit…he did have to concede…plain.

"How may I be of service to you?" he asked Miss Bonger.

"I wish to buy a painting," she said, smiling. "Something extraordinary and Andres tells me that you're the man to see."

"Well I thank my friend dearly for the recommendation, however, I fear that most of what you see here at Goupil will prove masterful, inspirational even—but…extraordinary? That is a whole different matter Madame."

Coyly, she replied, "Then you have nothing you can show me that I've asked for?"

Theo thought for a moment. He had, personally, been collecting certain works from certain artists at Le Chat (some for as cheap as a drink of absinthe on nights when artists found themselves broke). But it would be inappropriate for him to ask a proper lady to his apartment.

"I'll tell you what, Miss Bonger, I will take to Andres' flat several extraordinary canvases and you can see them there. If you like one of them…then we can discuss the arrangements. Is this acceptable to you?"

"Very much so," she smiled. "And now I'd like you to show me the rest of what Goupil has to offer. Of things… less-extraordinary."

Miss Bonger and her escort spent the better part of their afternoon walking round and round the well-lit, high-ceilinged gallery all the while chatting with Theo about art, the art world, and each other.

***

"Okay," Vincent continued, "Yesterday we met Christian, Obstinate, Pliable and Evangelical. So today we'll meet..." he pulled out a drawing of a nice strong colt tied to a coal cart..."Help."

The girl squealed, "I love hor-sees."

"Me too," said Tommy, "and that one there," he pointed to Vincent's drawing, "is the strongest one I've ever seen!"

"Yeah," added Jake. Mark just nodded.

"So Christian is going along with Pliable and they fall into the Slough of Despond..."

Marie asked, "What's that?"

Vincent realized it was no use trying to move on. Mark, Jake and Marie would need to hear the story from the beginning. So he began again. But he noticed that the kids responded best to the drawings

[especially—and again—to that of Evangelist].

He wondered what it was about that particular drawing that touched them so profoundly. He made a mental note to study the *it* later.

Once everyone was up to speed, Vincent proceeded with the colt drawing story:

"...and so Help said to Christian, who was sinking fast in the Slough of Despond —almost going under—drowning, like some of the miners have when the shafts have flooded..."

The children's eyes grew terrified.

"...but then Help whinnied and it sounded to Christian like he was saying: 'Stand up! Stand up for the love of God!' And that's when Christian felt, beneath his feet, that there was some firm ground...and he climbed out, slowly."

The children—and the grandmother—heaved sighs of relief. Vincent continued: "Then the colt pointed his hoof and whinnied, 'Why didn't you use the ford over there?' And Christian said that he did not know why. So Help replied, 'It was fear that nearly sunk you. The Slough of Despond is Fear and it drowns everyone who lets it.'"

Marie cried, "But I'm afraid of that story!"

Vincent smiled, "Well, Marie, now you know. There is nothing to fear. Help is there for you when you're afraid—because God is always there for you and when you believe in Him then Fear will never overcome you."

His time was already up. And he hadn't even gotten a chance to show the kids his last three drawings:
The Worldly Wiseman,
The Shining Gate (with its door covered in old bloodstains) and Goodwill. But there was always tomorrow.

As he tucked his drawings away and said goodbye to Jake, Mark and Marie, Tommy and Tommy's grandmother he promised to be back the next day to continue the story. At this, Jake, Mark and Marie all jumped up and ran outside. Tommy, however, stayed close and it seemed, to Vincent, as if he had something he wanted to say—or ask—but was having a difficult time with it. So he decided to help.
"Tommy?"
"Yes Father."
"Is there something you want to say?"
The boy pointed his big toe and ran it in a semi-circle on the floor in front of him. "Well…" the boy stammered, "I was wondering…if I could…keep your picture of Evangelist."
Vincent could see his grandmother paying attention as well. Even though he'd wanted to study the drawing himself (to see what seemed to make it so moving) he gave it to the boy without further hesitation. "Here you go, Tommy. I'm glad you like it so much."
The boy threw his arms around Vincent's waist. "Thank you! Thank you!" the boy cried.
While he walked back to his room Vincent wiped away his tears and silently prayed, "Thank you! Thank you Lord."
***

After such a good day of business Theo was in high spirits. When Messr Salis showed him to his table Theo asked for, instead of absinthe, a nice bottle of wine. When Messr Salis returned with a red. Theo asked if See was working, to which Salis nodded his head, but then replied, "Though I don't know for how much longer."

"How come?"

"Well...the customers don't like her so much."

"What!"

"Yes. And she can't sing. So there's not much use for her. Because she won't...well, you know. And I've tried talking to her. But she won't hear of it. Not to mention that I doubt she'd be very 'busy' even then."

"How can you say that!" Theo stood as if Salis had just insulted his own mother.

"Messr van Gogh. There is no need for all of this. She's a fine woman," he said, then under his breath "ugly..."

"What did you say?"

"Nothing. Nothing. I just say that she's a fine woman. Only, Le Chat may not be the place for her is all."

Theo was appeased enough to return to his seat. And...if truth were told, he didn't particularly care to ruin what had been—up to that moment—an exquisite day. However, amends were in order: "A drink with me, then, Salis?"

Salis sat. He never declined his patrons the sharing of their drink. And after a few moments silence—letting the red swill round cheeks and sweetly slip down throats, Salis felt it prudent (in light of seeing Theo's passion for the girl) to suggest that, perhaps, he might approach See—in order that she might become his mistress.

Had it been any other man—in any other place— decorum would have mandated Theo to take that suggestion as an effrontery. But...it was Le Chat Noir...and it was a stagegirl...and it was Paris in the time of, the dawning of, the Impressionists.

So when Salis stood, saying, "I'll send her to your table." Theo did not resist. After all, wasn't it his duty—being raised by a Protestant preacher—to assist those who'd fallen onto difficult times?

***

When Vincent returned to his room, which was in fact, a chicken-coop attached the back of one of the poorest miner's family's home (though the family had taken pains to make it clean for their minister) he was—at first—very happy to see…that his father had come to visit.

It did not take long for emotions to change. Indictments rained as if the springmist were falling atop the young evangelist's head.

His father raved: "How, after choosing such a menial vocation (after such a promising career in the family business— and worst, after proclaiming wanting to be a proper minister— and against wishes to go about things properly) could you, in fact, manage to fail even at a job considered unfit for people elevated no higher than the town drunkard?"

Vincent did not reply. There was a long silence.

"Is it true," Pastor Theodorus accused, "that you go around unwashed? Covered in filth?"

"Father, I minister to the miners *inside* the mines! How can I keep my clothes clean, or even my skin…and what does that matter? I am with them how they need me to be, where they need me to be…oh, Father, if you could only see how they suffer…and how the encouraging words of God ease their burdens then I know you'd…"

"And what about God's command that we be in the world, not of the world."

"Exactly! I am physically dirty but that does not matter to God. It's the purity of my love for Him that make the people hear my testimony."

"Vincent. You can not continue like this."

"But Father. Won't you please just come along with me to see what I've managed to do here? For instance, there are some children and I've made some sketches to go with Bunyan's…"

"Vincent! You have not heard me. You will **NOT** continue here and that is final. I can not have a son of mine behaving as you are! People are talking, Vincent! They're saying that you're mad and that I should have you put away because it's not right for a man of proper upraising to be carrying on in the ways that you are.

Even Reverend Rochedieu warned me that if you continued to downwardly move your residence—and mind you, Vincent, he was referring to the move you'd made from Peddler van der Haegen's place to Baker Denis's house—because he thought it was too close to the miners. Reverend Rochedieu considered *that* move ill-advised because of his belief that you must distance yourself from the lives of the miners, lest their ways corrupt you. And I defended you!

I said that the move was merely to save your feet from all the walking—as you were so passionate in your duties that you spent much time with the miners."

Pastor Theodorus, calmed a bit—lowered his head, "I even took his reprobation upon myself when he said that it is a poor reflection upon the parent when a child shows such weakness." Pastor Theodorus then looked at Vincent, continuing, "He was referring to a lack of character in a pastor who would take their own feet into consideration…if he knew all of this," he held his hands up, pedantically, and moved them circularly around the head {displaying the chicken-coop}.

Then, as if seized by the power of the Holy Spirit, Pastor Theodorus wildly threw his hands high above his head, flailing them about until his eyes managed to focus on a white chicken feather that had wedged itself into the fadedgray crack of wood forming the angle between the shed's wall and roof. "This! Vincent, is unacceptable."

"But Father. Why should I live any different from those to whom I minister?"

Theodorus shot up. "You are NOT a minister!"

And Vincent knew there was no use in fighting. His father, though a small parish minister, was part of something greater, something larger—something, perhaps, nefarious— and *that* something had determined: his time in the Borinage was at its end.

However, there was one: hope. So while assenting to his father's demands for him to quit the life of the Evangelist— he focused on Charles Hadden Spurgeon.

Charles Haden Spurgeon was a revivalist and Vincent determined (as he watched his father leave that afternoon) there was but one thing yet for him to do: he immediately traveled to London.

Vincent would not be at Tommy's house the next day, to see the looks upon the faces of Mark, Jake, Marie…Susan, Jason, Eli, Grant, and Melody
>   (all who'd heard about the story of Christian and wanted
>   to see the beautiful drawings)
or Tommy's grandmother
>   (who'd used the last bit of her coal, keeping the Father's
>   coffee hot…though he did not show)

or Tommy —who,
>   after they'd waited an hour—showed everyone the
>   drawing Vincent had given him of "Evangelist" and
did his best to tell the story he'd learned
of how Christian got sunk in stew
and thought…he'd get…eaten up by…a donkey…who kicked him so hard that his feet went superfast…
>   he made his hands go back and forth in front of him to
illustrate
…and then how Christian got to meet God.
***

See came to Theo's table. He offered her wine, but she refused. He explained to her her situation, that she was through at Le Chat, but she would not believe it. Not until Salis came and said it was so.

"So this is it?" she asked Salis.

"This is it. Make sure you put the costume back where you found it, eh?" and he gave her her final pay.

After that she was silent. She did take Theo up on his offer and drank in the dark bloody wine. About halfway through the bottle Theo saw Andres come through the door, but when he began his approach to their table, Theo ushered him away with his eyes.

Andres, having adjusted his focus to see See, gracefully redirected to another table—where several girls quickly appeared…all of them the kind who worked familiar and friendly with the code.

When Theo determined the wine had had time to take its effect he began. For Theo's mind was quick at working things out. It had taken but minutes (after Salis' revelation regarding See) for him to determine a foolproof plan to possess his Dutch Beauty. "So now," he asked as if he weren't interested in her reply, "What will you do?"

"There are other stages."

"To be sure," Theo maintained his aloof, "But everyone in Paris knows that what Salis gives 'the boot to' no one else wants."

"So rumors say. But I'm not afraid of rumors."

Theo raised his eyebrows. "Really?" he asked, his façade giving way to excitement.

"Really. And here's another thing:" See looked for Salis and, after making eye contact, raised her glass to him, "Good riddance!"

She gulped an almost-full glass.

Theo motioned, this time for absinthe and before the night had ended, with See still in her stage clothes and both in synesthesis, an agreement had been struck. See would live, rent-free, with Theo—platonically, he swore—until she could find herself proper work.

She swore he was the nicest man she'd ever met and revealed to Theo that she'd met some pretty nice men in her lifetime, "rich men," because her family had been well-off.

Merchants. She mentioned cotton and changes in the market. And how badly her father had felt having to send her away in order to work, in order that there'd be one less mouth to feed and hoping she'd send home a little money. She confessed how she'd secretly pined for the day she'd be free of the middleclass life
  —the downwardly mobile middleclass that she found to
  mean nothing except asphyxiation—
"…and…and…" she slurred, "Stupid!"
  Theo, much more able to contain his spirits, drank what she said in—deeply…and had already seen the way he'd take—to find himself inside her bed.
***

Vincent arrived at Victoria Station, London, and quickly made his way through (what was then) the industrial capital of the world. A world imbrued with as much wealth as poverty. A city where he'd met his mentor—and friend—
Thomas {Reverend Slade-Jones}.

It was near-late night when there came upon Rev. Slade-Jones' door a rapping. When he opened it, for a moment he stared—without speaking a word—as if his mind searched its nooks to identify the being standing before him. And then, those eyes, that fiery hair. "My God," he thought, "Vincent?" "Come in, come in," he said.
Looking out into the dark sky, before enclosing the young man within his home, he noticed that the blackblue was lit with blinking stars...and that it was, unseasonably, cold. He drew his robe closer around himself and withdrew inside. "Vincent," he said softly, as he thought his wife and children were still asleep—not knowing they all were listening from the second story landing—"What brings you here...at this time of night?"
"You must help me. I don't know what to do! It seems impossible and I don't know where to turn."
"Slow down, boy. Slow down. Here," he patted the sofa, "sit and tell me all about it."
They talked into the hours of peddler cartwheels beginning their clickety ticks atop cobbles.
"So, Thomas, you understand my situation then?"
The man sighed. He'd been an evangelist long enough to know the power of the church. And...he knew Vincent's father.
He never would forget the first time he met Pastor Theodorus van Gogh. The man, utilizing what seemed to be a great internal effort, had explained the absolute insolence of his son, Vincent
(Pastor Theodorus told Reverend Slade-Jones of how Vincent had thrown his—his own father's—religious tract upon a blazing fire).
To comfort him, Thomas said that all youth tend to rebel—and that the act he described was simply an indicator that Vincent would soon find, for himself, God's path.

But Pastor Theodorus was not easily consoled. He went on to explain the other odd behaviors of his son: all that he'd witnessed. And by the end of their conversation Reverend Slade-Jones thought that, perhaps, the elder minister was correct about his son's instability. The stories he'd been told did seem to reveal a young man riddled with strangeness. But when Reverend Slade-Jones offered to pray with Pastor Theodorus (having full confidence in the power of Biblical prayer), the elder minister refused stating that he had much to do (what with making arrangements for his unmanageable son).

"However," Pastor van Gogh replied, "I would be deeply grateful to you if you would keep an eye on him while he is in London. He has expressed a desire to enter the clergy—however was found unfit—and so he has determined to explore other venues of ministry."

Reverend Slade-Jones could not help but feel the sting of the patriarch's innuendo.

"Vincent," Thomas said, "You have chosen a very difficult path."
"Yes, but Christ tells us that His path is difficult."
"True. But I am concerned for you. How will you survive? The ministry in the Borinage paid nothing."
"Not in monetary ways, no...but my God, Thomas, if you could see what I've seen! Those beautiful people just waiting for God to deliver them..."
"Yes, Vincent, I understand. I really do. But you still have to eat and, I believe, it was your earthly father...who supported you in *those* ways?"

Vincent's lowered his eyes. "Yes."
"And he has forbidden you to continue your ministry?"

Vincent's chin quivered. "Yes."
"Then, my boy," Reverend Slade-Jones replied, putting his hand on Vincent's shoulder, "Not even God asks you to starve."
"But there just has to be a way! Can't you speak to the Board? Make them see?"

Thomas rose. Walked to his desk, withdrew a letter and read aloud:

Dear Reverend Slade-Jones,

I believe my son, Vincent, will be visiting you soon. Please be advised that he has been formally discharged from his ministerial post in the Borinage. This decision was made unanimously by the governing body and is irreversible. Should Vincent appeal to you for assistance, I humbly beseech you to do the kindest act: discourage him from further continuing in this vocation. It has been, unequivocally, found that—for this endeavor—he is most unfit.

With a Handshake,
Pastor Theodorus van Gogh.

Vincent sat, stunned. How could his father do this? What would he do now? Thomas could see the maelstrom behind the young man's tearing eyes.
"If there was some way to support yourself—perhaps you could still minister."
"You mean—outside the church?"
"Sure, Vincent. God doesn't care what church you go to, or associate with. He cares about you! He cares about His ministry."
Vincent's spirit visibly lifted. Thomas smiled, slapped Vincent's shoulder.
"Besides, the Word of God is filled with the suffering of His workers. Perhaps this is your destiny."
Vincent's chest took in a big breath. "Yes, Thomas. Yes! I bet the people there would give me food—though they're nearly starving themselves…because God promises that just as the sparrows and animals and plants get what they need, He will do nothing less for us."
"Yes, Brother. That's it!"
Vincent rose, enthusiastically, shook the man's hand and swore he'd be the very best testament to God as was humanly possible. And he was nearly out the door when he suddenly remembered, "Here," Vincent said, pulling a book from the inside of his   thinly/threadbare%&holey   jacket."
"What's this?"

"It's by Emile Zola. *Germinal.* Have you read it?"

"No. Is it good?"

"After you read it you'll understand this all so much more."

And with that, he was gone—into the darkest hour of night.

***

In the meantime, a rich van Gogh uncle died and this…this put a different spin on things. For if there was one thing Theo aspired for, most earnestly—it was wealth. But inheritances have ways of splitting themselves into such dividends as to be hardly drops in puddles (particularly if the puddles are of the stylish Parisian kinds and the drops to be divided in thirds: his, Vincent's and little Cor's). So a trip was planned to the homeland…but not before Theo laid claim to a different stake: his Dutch Beauty had not yet awakened from the sleep (he'd guaranteed it deep, via excessive absinthe).

He pricked the inside of his ring finger

(making sure not to leave a visible mark)

and bled himself, strategically, upon the sheet.

Then he left her there to wonder the nature of (the origins of) the scarlet~crimson. He quickly exited the bedroom (bags packed—and without a word to See) for the train station: money took precedence over sex.
***

Once back in the Borinage, Vincent quickly discovered that his beliefs had been correct:

> his father had sent a letter requesting his immediate return home and that his monthly income would be thenceforth suspended (and would continue to be so until he came home)

and

> he found that the miners (the miners Vincent had comforted in their times of need, to whom he'd given his winter clothes when they were in want—from freezing, and to whom he'd given his last bit of money when their children starved)—in fact, fed him...when they could.

However, the weather was changing. It was growing colder.

The family who'd lent Vincent their chicken-coop insisted he pay or leave—not out of maliciousness...they needed the space for the chickens (for the fowl had been living with them inside the house while Vincent had had the coop) and, with winter coming, they felt the chickens needed to be back where chickens roosted best.

Vincent understood. He went throughout the miner's town...but everyone was so crowded, so miserable, that without the ability to exchange money

{$=food|heat}

he found the people quite unable to burden another unpleasantry—or to feed one more hungry soul.

He slept where he could: mainly tall grass and haystacks. When the wind was particularly fierce, he slept behind buildings to keep the wind's fury from piercing his skin with bits of coal as small and biting as sand. Perhaps, once a week (sometimes up to thrice) he was given a little bread.

Yet he knew he could always count on Tommy's grandmother. She'd keep him warm—and only charged that he tell more of Bunyan's story.

He still went into the mines and preached the Gospel of Christ. He still tried to minister to the people, but he noticed that the longer he lived as he was living—without even a place to lay his head...or to clean his body...the people—the miners themselves—seemed less willing.

This troubled Vincent, deeply. And it made him ponder whether or not the choice he'd made was, in fact, hurting God's cause. Could it have been his own self—selfishness—that drove him to ministry? Was his decision carnal?

This scenario would have gone on (for God only knew how long)—but did only...until the new minister came.

He was sparkling clean, immaculately neat, and lived—as one might guess—with the baker, Messr Denis.

Vincent was convinced that, in spite of the young man's decided goodlooks and, apparently, well-bred manners that the miners would not forget all he'd done for them...how he'd sacrificed for them just so they could come to know Jesus in a personal way.

Vincent, however, grossly overestimated the ability for sentimentality amongst the starvingly poor. They could not afford high ideals. And when the new minister came, armed with free bread—even cheese on Sundays—it was as if Vincent had never even existed.

That is, except for Tommy and his grandmother, who gladly—enthusiastically—embraced Vincent's every visit. Yet, even they could not afford to reject what they so badly needed. So when Vincent came

—that day—

the day he was just finishing near-to-the-end of Bunyan's story about the Deceiver

(and, not surprisingly, Vincent's drawing looked rather a lot like the new minister—wearing {instead of the apparel of Evangelical} a Pastor's habit)

and Tommy's grandmother offered Vincent a slice of bread...and cheese Vincent knew exactly where they'd come from and rose from their table...never to return.

Ironically, it so happened, that as he was closing the door behind him—in the throes of piercing betrayal—someone appeared. It was his little brother, Theo, come to him [under the guise of] to deliver: bad news.
***

When See awoke she felt as if someone had hit her over the head with a lead pipe. Her ears rang. Her teeth itched. And then she noticed. Her clothes had been stripped and there was an ever-so-small stain of blood on the sheet between her legs.

She leapt up, grabbed the topsheet and wrapped it round herself. "Where are my clothes?" She was alone. She ran to the armoire. Everything was there, neatly hung or neatly folded.

She wildly looked around the room then threw the sheet to the ground and dressed as quickly as she could. Once dressed, she pinned her hair up. Now, at least, she was ready to face the man who'd done this to her. It would be too much shame to do so, naked.

She sat on the couch, trying to remember the night before but it was all blank. Like someone had erased everything from after when she sat at Theo's table and drank that dark red wine.

She felt woozy. And then was seized with gagging. She barely made it to the washbasin before throwing up—it was all yellow bile and dry heaves. Her forehead was clammy. Her legs ached and her belly felt swollen.

She cried. For it was not supposed to be like this. Yes, she'd come to Paris and—in defiance of her parents—did not take a 'respectable' position, but did that mean she deserved to be violated? Didn't girls, even those at Le Chat Noir, have the right choose…with their own bodies?

That was when she noticed, atop Theo's writing desk, a small purse and a note:

My Dearest See,

You've made me exceedingly happy. As to our agreement, here is the amount I owe you. I will be out of town for no more than a week. I have family business to attend to.

Yours,
Theo.

She opened the purse. It contained more than she'd have earned at Le Chat Noir in an entire year. She set it back. And cried more.

Eventually, she looked around the apartment, with its nice things, and thought, "It could be worse. Obviously, he's in love with me *and* has means. Perhaps this will be a good match. Still! I didn't want to marry so young…but what choice do I have…now?"

Thus, considering the limitations of her options, See determined that Theo and she would need to announce their engagement, soon.

For See knew enough of about life—and the girls from Le Chat Noir had informed her further—that it would not be wise to wait…lest she find herself, in the next month, unable to bleed.

***

Chapter: The Second Betrayal

"Brother!" Vincent cried. Grabbing Theo, heartily, and hugging him long.

"Vincent," he replied, pushing himself away and brushing

(what he could, visibly, see was his brother's filth)

clean his
new suit.

But Vincent would not be dissuaded. Even in starvation he was the larger and stronger of the two and so succeeded in drawing Theo close again, slapping him on the back and covering him with the fondest salutations.

Helpless to do otherwise, Theo waited until this was done then set about to the business at hand. "Vincent," Theo said, "We must talk."

"Yes, yes, Brother, we must! I have such important things to tell you! The miners here…well before that darned minister…"

"Now just stop!" Theo yelled.

Vincent had never heard his little brother yell. It shocked him—and worried him. "Brother, are you okay?"

"No, Vincent, I'm not okay. And no one at home is okay either."

"What's going on? Is Father ill? Mother?"

"No, they're fine, but everyone is exceedingly concerned about you."

"Me? Why?"

Theo, dramatically, moved his eyes up and down his brother's figure. "Must you ask? Just look at yourself!"

"I know. I know I must look a mess."

"A mess! A mess! You look like, well, worse than that—like a homeless, desolate, skeleton of a man and this *must* stop."

"Father sent you didn't he?"

"Yes…partially. But I came because, Vincent,"

and he made the greatest effort to breathe through his
mouth in order to be saved from inhaling his brother's
overwhelming bodystench as he quickly [mechanically]
embraced him,

"you're my brother."

Vincent smiled. Tears came, then, easy. Even Theo's heart could not but be touched. It was apparent, then, how much he'd suffered.

"Vincent," Theo's voice came soft and silky, "come home."

"But I've a ministry here," Vincent waved his hands over the grayblack of one of the poorest coal mining camps in the country.
"But you don't." Theo said, pointing—
        the new minister was, at that very moment, approaching
        the brothers...as if entering [stage right] on cue,
"He is the minister."

        When Vincent looked up
{for he'd pushed his face into the palms of his hands}
        he saw—in a stream of sunlight—a figure in white
approaching him. He could not see the face
        but it seemed like one of Bunyan's Shining Ones
from the Celestial City.
        Hunger had taken cruel-hold of his senses...making him
see what he hoped. And hear...what he hoped to hear:
        that his beloved miners would be safely left unto the
        hands of a great deliverer who promised to minister to
        them...just as Christ had.
***

The first thing See did that day, after her resolution, was to write her parents in Holland and announce the engagement. After all, the more she read Theo's letter, the clearer it all became. Beginning with:
"Dearest."
Obviously affection.
"You've made me exceedingly happy,"
had to mean that she'd consented to marry him
(which explained her allowing what had occurred...to occur)
and not only was he glad but was
"exceedingly" so.
However, the
"Agreement—and amount I owe you"
did bother her for a while, but she quickly dismissed this as, perhaps, some sort of reference to...a reverse dowry?
Yet it couldn't be bad, for he signed it,
"Yours,"
which re-affirmed it for See: they'd become engaged and she couldn't wait for her fiancée to return from wherever it was he'd gone.

There were a few 'details' that evaded See and frustrated her attempts in writing her parents. For example: she did not know how to spell Theo's last name. But she quickly remedied this, after finding a stack of letters to Theo from his relatives (which she read—every one of them thereby gleaning a great deal of information).
She told her parents that the date of the wedding was yet to be determined but that her intended was from a respectable family. She said that his father was a pastor and that he had, rather high, connections in the Admiralty and the art world. She wrote, "And he's doing quite well for himself also so he will be able to adequately support our family."
She smiled. For although she'd wanted to wait to have a family, the thought of it now—now that the choice had been taken from her—surprisingly pleased her. She rubbed her belly and wondered if...
"Ever Yours," she signed and hurried to the postal clerk.

On the way the smells of a bakery wafted the air. She could never before afford such luxuries—(neither to her purse...nor her figure} as all women knew that the latter was their greatest asset—but now things were different. She was to be married...and she had money...and the hot croissant's buttery, flaky flesh tasted like nothing she'd ever known.

If only she'd known.

***

In the Borinage, Theo prepared his brother. The physical leaving did not take much for he had about him very few physical possessions. However the emotional, spiritual, and intellectual preparedness proved much more difficult.

It seemed that, after seeing the "Shining One from the Celestial City," Vincent was convinced it had been a sign that God wanted him to stay and preach. The minister (who'd been the one with the mistaken identity of "Shining One") assured Vincent that it was merely his hunger and physical degradation that made him see such a vision. Vincent then cursed the minister saying that he was "The Deceiver" and obviously didn't know his Bible.

"For even Jesus said that great things come from fasting," Vincent screamed at the man.

Theo, while Vincent railed the young evangelist, told Vincent to sign something. Vincent did as he was told, for his heart was in this throat with preaching Gospel.

Theo smiled at the preacher. "Excuse him, Father, he's not well."

When Vincent heard this,
his face took on the horrific
—as if Abel's just before Cain's betrayal—
"What do you mean, Theo? I am perfectly well."

Theo smiled, again, at the preacher. "You see. I'm sure you've received the correspondence from my father...our father?"

"Yes, Messr van Gogh. I understand. May I help you?"

The young man tried to help Theo assist Vincent to standing.

Vincent responded in rage, "The two of you! It's become clear! Oh, how the heart pains when one's own brother..."

Theo, raising his eyebrows in innocence, "Brother, I don't know what you're talking about."

"Don't call me Brother! No brother of mine would do as you've done!"

"But Vincent," Theo cried, "I've done, nothing."

Theo quickly slid the paper inside his satchel.

"God forgive you both!" With that, Vincent tore from the men's
grips and walked away
     and away
        and 100 kilometers later
            —after some wondered if he'd ended up
        dead—he rose
            (from the mystery of his ashes)
                to climb his family's home's
            doorstep, proclaiming he'd had a
            vision:
        on his journey
(his Christian walk—with a heavy, heavy burden upon his back)
     he'd found, in one of his pockets, the drawing of the
coalcolt. And he remembered how his picture of Evangelist
had touched those who'd seen—those who'd needed to see.
     Still…he walked on
(many, many days without food or water or comfort)
     until finally God revealed to him
(in his moment of greatest physical torment and emotional pain)
this:
     "I have given you a gift. Praise Me,
        the Father|Son|Holy Spirit,
    with it."

To the utter surprise (shock and dismay) of his family (minus
Theo, who'd already returned to Paris) Vincent then
proclaimed:
        "I'm to be an artist!"
***

In Paris, See waited. True to his word, Theo returned within the week. It was…at first awkward. For even though the experience of having his Dutch Beauty throw her arms around his neck {smothering his face
(and lips) with kisses} pleased him, he'd not anticipated what came next. See told him she'd informed her parents of their engagement.

Theo's eyes grew wide.

> See chattered on about the shops she'd visited, about the wedding plans she'd made and asked how much she might expect to spend on their special day. And if they'd honeymoon abroad.

Theo made no reply.

> See was naïve: she kept rambling on about the bakery she'd been to and how, after eating a croissant, she spoke to the baker about a cake.

Theo rose, went to the door and exited.

> A horrified look crossed her face. Reason flooded in.
> "My God!" she cried aloud, "I'm ruined!"

Theo went directly to Le Chat.

> It was, in fact, the end of that day and Andres was

already sitting at their table sipping his absinthe and enjoying the girls (who were displaying their 'wares' for him from the stage).

"Theo!" Andres exclaimed, "Where have you been?"

> Theo needed no further invitation. He sat and told his

friend everything (except the part of his bloody deception, leaving Andres to believe—like See—that they'd 'known' each other that night).

"Old Man, what rotten luck," Andres sighed. "And now she thinks you're going to marry her?"

"Yes. She's told her parents. What am I going to do?"

> Andres grew serious. "Is there any way she could

be…you know…in that way?"

"Oh no no. Absolutely not."

Andres harumpf'd, "How can you be so sure?"

By then Salis had brought Theo his absinthe (he liked to, personally, deliver at least one drink to his very regular customers). Theo took an exceptionally large sip…and waited…for the ever-so-slight halo to begin around the footlight he was staring out. It's appearance gave him courage. "Andres. She is *not* with child."

Andres dropped the subject. He preferred, especially when beginning to enjoy his refreshment, not to ponder unpleasant things and so changed the subject. "I hear you met my little sister," Andres smiled.

One of the new girls, a redhead rumored to be from Spain, flipped her ruffled skirt edge in Andres' direction. He remained wondering how much it would cost him {to see all of what her costume contained} when Theo replied, "Oh yes. She made a rather large purchase."

"I know. I sent her to you."

Theo looked, intently, at his friend, "Are you scheming?" Andres smiled again, a bit more slyly. "Me? Would I do something like that?"

It was no secret to Theo that Andres' family had a respectable income. One born from manufacturing that grew into comfortable middleclass—a child that longed for legitimization—of which

(although on the low-end of the scale) connection with the clergy class could provide.

Theo contemplated (rather calculated), weighing the benefit to what he'd seen of the young woman at his store. She was rather plain in looks (sort of boyish) and, it seemed to him, acted pretentious. But there would be compensation…worth considering, which was exactly what Theo did the whole of the night as he and his friend took in the shows of young feminine flesh.

See wanted nothing more than the reassurance that everything was right between them. So later, when Theo clutched the neck of her dress and thrust his body atop her, See made no resistance. She knew. Her salvation wrested Theo's pleasure, in her.

Yet when she woke in the morning (Theo having risen early and gone) she thought it rather odd...that there—again—on the sheet lay a tiny pool of blood.

***

"Father," Vincent cried, "Nobody has understood me! You—
and them!" he flailed his arms at some invisible circumscribing
force engulfing him, "You all think I'm a madman because I
wanted to be a **_true_** Christian? I want to **_serve_** God!"
"Now Vincent," Theodorus, shaking his head in a manner of
condescension, "I think you exaggerate."
"Exaggerate! I was turned out like a dog. It was you yourself
that said I was causing a scandal. Was it not?"
"Yes. And you were…"
"That is a lie, Father!"

Vincent's mother, who (although slightly older than his
father) preferred peaceful and joyous scenes of domesticity,
quickly exited the scene. Vincent watched her set up her easel
in the yard; she was painting the wildflowers in watercolor.

Theodorus (more because of slander than for his wife's
concern) stormed out and stood beside his wife.

Vincent watched the man and the woman. He wondered
what it was that ever made a man take a wife—or vice versa—
for in his parents he'd never seen the slightest display of
affection…of anything other than the traversing of distance
when one would move away and the other followed. Ways
varied only by which of the two took turns leading.

Vincent saw his mother's lips moving. His father
(shaking his head like a schoolboy receiving his lesson)
returned. "Vincent."
"Yes Father?"
"You must not speak so disrespectfully to me again. It is a
sin…and it upsets your mother."
"Yes. You're correct. Forgive me. And I forgive you too."
"For what am I to be forgiven?"
"For not understanding what you've done."

Vincent took up his drawing pad, but before he exited
> [to go somewhere far away from his mother, his
> father, his family…and home]
he said, "I only tried to relieve some of the misery in those
wretched lives. Now…I don't know what I'm going to do.
Perhaps, Father, you were right in saying that I am idle and
useless on this earth."
> He assumed complete sorrow, then
> closed the door behind himself.

Theodorus,
watching his son's frame
>   (having become a near-skeleton from his days of
>   evangelism in what his son called "The country of
>   oleanders and sulphur sun")

was seized with an uncontrollable weeping. Such that when Vincent's sister (the eldest of his three sisters) found her father crying she cursed her eldest brother, "I wish he'd never come home!" To which Theodorus replied, clutching her dress sleeve, "You must never say such a thing. He is not well."

"He's selfish! It's always about him and what he wants, what he thinks, what he believes. He lords it over everyone in this house, including you, Father, and it's just not right!"

"I know. I know. But we must do what's best for those less fortunate than us."

"Less fortunate! He's gotten to do everything he's ever wanted and you pay for it. How is that less fortunate?"

"You don't understand."

"Oh, but I do. I really do, Father. Theo has explained it all to me."

"Has he? What has he told you?"

"That Vincent has already spent all his inheritance."

"What!"

>   Now the man stood in search to see if he could find his
son's figure somewhere off in the distance.

"Yes. He gave it all away to those peasant miners."

"No!"

"Yes. And worse."

"There's more?"

"Well, Theo says that Vincent's been spending time with some of the women miners. And that maybe that's why he's been acting so strange. Because sometimes those women give men things that make them crazy."

"Anna! I will not have you talk of such things!"

"Fine, Father. But Theo says that maybe Vincent should be put in an asylum."

>   "Dear God,"

Pastor Theodorus thought, watching his wife painting,

>   "...it would break her heart"

but said to his daughter, "Leave me" and she obeyed. She
didn't waste a single moment before reporting [in letter]
to her brother {closer brother, Theo},
what had just taken place.
***

Goupil's mimicked a crypt. Nothing stirred. Hour upon hour passed. Theo walked to the front door's glass, wiped it with a cloth, smiled at passersby and silently prayed that the day would miraculously end. When, in walked Miss Bonger (and her escort), "Are you open for business, Messr van Gogh," the young woman asked.

"Oh yes. Yes." Excitement poured as if the three words were explicatives.

"Very good."

The two women stood near the door, waiting for Theo to usher them in. Moments ticked by. Both women grew, visibly, uncomfortable with Theo's, seeming, lack of propriety.

But it wasn't Theo's fault. He was stuck, in his mind—like a repeating phrase—seeing the stage footlight's glimmering haze and the resounding idea, Bonger's idea, that he should engage his sister.

Miss Bonger, putting her kerchief to her mouth, cleared her throat. This stimulus proved enough. Theo awoke from his stupor and, reassuming all his charm and vigor, led the ladies through. "I am sorry to say, Miss Bonger," he said as they walked, "that there is nothing additional here to show you, since you came last week."

"Jo, please," Miss Bonger replied. "I think less formality is in order…as my brother has conveyed to me the solidity…of your resolutions."

Theo's eyes grew wide. "He did?"

"Oh yes. And I believe it would be best if you met my parents straight away."

"You…do?"

Jo, ever-so-slightly, threw back her head. Her eyes narrowed. Her heart filled with suspicion. "And…" she continued, "Andres told me you are familiar with where we live?"

The truth was that Andres had never told Theo, specifically, where he lived—or maybe he had…on one of those nights…brimmed with absinthe…but for the life of him he could not recall. And for many, many moments he stood there, saying nothing at all, but rather murmuring—like one made dumb by the cutting out of the tongue—until Jo's doubts took firm foothold…and forced her to do something that (even to herself) seemed surprising. "It does not matter," she said.

Her escort's eyes filled with condemnation.
"You're not an honest man, then."

Theo was about to argue, but Jo held up her hand to him.
"It's best we know the truth about each other. I am not pretty…and you are deceitful. There it is. I live with my parents…"

And she proceeded to give him her address before she and her escort exited. Theo, again alone, pondered what exactly had happened. That was when See suddenly appeared. "Dear God," Theo thought, "What do I do now?!"

To his surprise, and rescue, there came a telegram.
***

When Vincent returned,
        having made several sketches of
his father's parish,
the fields with their crows
and the graveyard
            (much like the picture that hung above his father's
            rectory's desk)
it was after dusk,
        (nearing night)
he found his entire family waiting for him, including Theo.
        Vincent looked from one set of eyes to the next.
Vincent's eyes
        (those of the eldest)
drew to those of the youngest
        [which belonged to Cor, or Cornelius]
who was merely thirteen years old
            (and the only one of Pastor Theodorus' children who had
            similar interests to those of of Pastor Theodorus' Navy
            Admiral|Brother—in that Cor loved everything military)
and whose expression conveyed utter boredom.
        It was what some might call 'an intervention' as the
father expressed his dismay, disgust, exasperation and
hopelessness over what he'd learned—that his eldest son had
squandered his inheritance.
        Anna and Theo shook their heads at him in near
synchronization.
Vincent's mother and his sisters Lies and Wil
        (their proper names being: Elisabeth and Wilhelmina,
        respectively. And Wilhelmina being named in honor of
        the King)
were the epitome of sympathy. For whether they expressed it
(which they did not, except amongst themselves—the three)
they had long-admired the selflessness of Vincent's personality.
        Naturally, it was to these six eyes that Vincent looked for
support. But found, as with his beloved Borinage miners, they
were helpless—in the face of such calculating opposition—to
do anything but remain silent.

"So," Vincent's father continued, "I've decided there is a choice
to be made Vincent. You must either go to an asylum...I've

been told there is an acceptable one in Gheel...or, because of Theo's position in the Art world, and your expressed desire to be an artist, you are to be put under his care."
Vincent screamed. Then pointed his shaking finger at his brother.
"He's the Deceiver. I tell you all!"
Theodorus stood. It seemed as if he would strike his son, "Enough! You will do as I say."
Vincent sucked in a deep breath, arched his back, and was silent for a moment, then cried.
Theo grinned a grin more akin to a sneer because he'd been living in his brother's shadow for years
(particularly regarding their father. For, in spite of Vincent being a zealot, he was still a spiritualist. He had forsaken the world of commerce—the world that their father had always secretly

/\/\/\/\/\/\/\/\/\/\/\/\/\/\/\
| sometimes openly, |
|yet always within the|
[confines of his home]

condemned ~Theo's world~ as 'an evil' of mankind). But now the tides had shifted. Theo had finally managed to oust his brother from his favored position. Theo soaked up each tense moment that passed between the family's patriarch and its prodigal son. He had not, however, planned on his mother's intercession.
"Vincent," she said, softly, "Come with me." And she led her eldest son outdoors...into the dark, starry night.
Pastor Theodorus sent everyone to bed. Even Theo, who—though giving much protest—obeyed.
Left alone, in the room where all his family had just been, he looked out the window to see his wife, pointing to the stars
—and to the spire of the church—
holding the arm of her eldest boy
(to whom her heart was so particularly warm...as he'd been the one to survive...whereas her first Vincent had died)

71

and there was a part of the man of Pastor Theodorus van Gogh...deeper than he liked to admit...that was— ever-so-slightly—jealous.

That night, Vincent did not sleep under his father's roof. After his mother had left his side he remained in the warm air
—for it was, by then, a mild spring—
and watched how every so often
...if one were diligent and did not look away...
a brilliant light streaked the sky.

He prayed to God, asking Him to fight this fight for him. Praying that he be obedient to his Father's will
—whether or not his Father's will
and his father's will were the same—
and still, by the time the pink—
then orange—
then yellow—
then white of the coming sunrise lightened
        the Prussian blue of darkness,
he did not feel God's intervention.
He could not know that his mother had finally found her voice that night beside her husband where she pled Vincent's case.

Theo, too, spent a sleepless night. Much was riding upon what was to be and he'd done his best to hedge his bets. If his brother was institutionalized then he (being the one member of Pastor Theodorus' family still in the world of business) would, most likely, be given control of Vincent's share of the van Gogh estate
        (for there was wealth amongst the elder van Goghs, particularly Uncle Cent who, although still quite living, wouldn't last...forever).

And, unbeknownst to the family (other than Pastor Theodorus) it had been Theo's suggestion of Gheel that formed the father's idea of placing Vincent in the asylum there.

And, unbeknownst to everyone (including the father), Theo's motive in having Vincent placed in Gheel was that, once admitted, the residents, typically, lived short lives.

On the other hand, if his brother were to be placed under Theo's personal care then, in addition to receiving his brother's inheritance, their father would (most likely) send Theo Vincent's monthly allowance (to cover his 'care').

Pastor Theodorus also spent a sleepless night; taking into consideration the words of his wife—who swore that if he institutionalized her son, there would be hell to pay.

His mind was tormented between versions of Hell:

her hell,

Vincent's hell,

God's hell. His hell?

With all that damnation the poor man felt absolutely incapable of praying so he simply lay, wide-eyed, and stared at the ceiling, swearing that the lights formed demons —dancing, jeering demons—all waiting for him to make that one 'fatal' pact...with the Devil.
***

There was a knock at the door. See saw that it was a man she recognized, but had forgotten his name. She opened the door.
"Andres," he said, kissing her hand and bowing, "I believe we've met...Le Chat."
She blushed. She was trying to forget the life she'd led. "Of course. Come in," she replied, spreading her hand in a grand gesture.
Andres eyed her figure and laughed, aloud. See was, he reported later to Theo, visibly hurt
{but quickly recovered her composure and offered him tea}.
He refused and said that she needn't bother herself with such pleasantries. That he'd come on Theo's behalf...to ask her to leave.
See became indignant, ordered him to leave.
Andres refused. And more—he began to strip off his clothes.
See screamed, "You get out! Get out this instant!"
"Or what," he laughed, "You'll call the police? Now that *would* be funny."
He was already naked when See ran to the corner of the room. She stared at the place where the two walls connected|knowing that, beneath the colored paper unity, the walls' wood would always remain<>separate.
Andres came up behind her, put his hands round her waist. There was no place for her to go. "You just don't understand it yet. Do you?"
See was crying.
"You're nothing but a whore. Theo's whore."
See turned, like a trapped cat, and clawed Andres' face, deep. He slapped her, hard, in return and she fell to the floor. He grabbed her by her hair's crown and dragged her to the bed, throwing back the blankets—then he saw the sheet.
"Are you indisposed?"
She clenched her teeth. She would not give him anything that he could not take.
"Is this your time?" he demanded.

She stood firm, and tall, and dignified in her silence. So he pulled her underclothes off. There was no linen there to catch blood.

He laughed. Wholeheartedly.

See's façade began to crumble. No one could be expected to be so strong.
"You were a virgin!"

He slapped his naked hip.

Her tears then greatly released, down her cheeks, into the crack between her lips and along the curve of her throat.

He tossed her onto the bed, then, and did that which he pleased.
***

The cock's crow brought the van Gogh family to face
what had begun the night before: Vincent's fate was to be
decided, early.

His mother kept her careful eye trained between her
husband and her son. Theodorus tried to ignore the woman,
but found his own gaze gravitating to what he was trying to
avoid. And still, as he traveled downstairs he did not know
what his answer would be.

Vincent, sitting—
straight|backed
          with eyes staring
past everyone and anything waited
          —like a convict (or saint)—
to see what his outcome would be.

Theo hung back, sitting atop the stairs.
"Vincent," Pastor Theodorus finally spoke
          (waiting for his son's acknowledgement)
but Vincent (having already determined to harden his heart
towards his father's words)—
would not give him the satisfaction of his eyes
...or his faith...
or anything except his obedience.

So after an awkward silence
          (filled with Vincent's mother's eyes increasingly intent on
          seeking out her husband's eyes {that grew, intentionally,
          more evasive})
Pastor Theodorus continued, "Vincent...I've decided..."
          Pastor Theodorus thought to himself: "What am I going
          to say? What's to be done? God please don't abandon
          me! I need Your help now more than ever..."
          {and before he knew what was coming out of his
          mouth—it came}
"...you're to go to the Hague and study art with our relation,
Mauve. I will send your allowance..."

Theo cried out, "What!"

His mother put her finger to her lips and, effectively, shushed her middle-son's objection.

However silenced, Theo determined his intentions would not, so easily, be thwarted. Things had not gone as he'd planned...but there had to be a way. It would just take some time...to figure it all out.

Meanwhile, after Andres had dressed he left See. Once again alone—in Theo's apartment. Only then, armed with the horror of what she'd just been forced to live she took in her hand the only weapon left her—pen. She wrote, introducing herself and announcing her engagement to their son; addressed: Pastor van Gogh. It was promptly posted.
***

Vincent found himself returning to The Hague
      (as he'd been there before…before…a lifetime
      before when he thought he was destined to follow
      the family business: dealing in the trade of art).
He'd accepted that his life's course of events was, in fact,
God's will for him and he was obedient to his father's wishes.
He immediately sought out his cousin's, Jet's, husband: Anton
Mauve.
      Anton Mauve was hardly an ideal mentor. In fact, had
his father known the fits of melancholia that Anton suffered, he
probably would not have suggested his son's tutelage under
him
      (though the suggestion had hardly seemed 'conscious'
      on his part).

When Anton opened his door and saw Vincent
      {still rather skeletal|
he frowned, slightly, then slapped him on the back and ushered
him in.
      Jet was sitting in the morning room (working on a
needlepoint that she quickly set aside) and warmly greeted her
cousin. It had been years since they'd seen him—and…oh, the
rumors they'd heard!
      Over tea the three discussed art, particularly the art
world, and how—although improved over the early '70s, there
was still as a sort of ominous fog (a remnant of France's Bloody
Week) that seemed to have a hold over Art. Plus sales weren't
good. Yet when Vincent expressed concern for Anton's
compensation, they both assured them that they were quite
well provided for.
      Vincent explained his situation (albeit
abbreviated&edited). Anton agreed to help him with his artistic
development, but not as a pupil…not as regular as that (for
Anton disclosed that his nerves would not tolerate that sort of
rigor). Rather Anton would instruct him as time and necessity
warranted. On those stipulations…he'd be there, for Vincent.
      Anton gave him a little money (to secure a place to
stay—in lieu of making an offer for him to room with them).
This was good enough for Vincent. He left them and checked

into a hotel. His first order of business was to find, by means of comparison, the cheapest accommodations available…and to draw.

      While he searched, he drew
the hotel,
the buildings around it,
the streets he'd walked until he'd gone near to where the town ended—
to where the dunes and trees began—in a place called Schenweg,
where he found what he called 'his studio'
(but what others, such as his father…or brother, would call a shack)
and he made himself, there, very happy.
***

Theo must have—just—arrived ahead of the telegram from his parents. He was, in fact, trying to console the near-hysterical See when a knock at the door came.

After reading the terseness of his father's message he vented his rage at its source: it would be days before the swelling reduced enough for See to be able to open her left eye.
***

Vincent visited Anton Mauve as often as he was allowed (which was to say that there were many days in between each tutorial). Vincent was exceedingly glad to receive suggestions, as he had—with the same determination as he'd been an evangelical—committed himself to Art…for God.

Anton was a man of strong opinions and held little back, with regard to criticism…of other people's work—particularly of Vincent's (as he did not feel Vincent's work was 'work'—or vocation—as much as it was…perhaps…a fancy).

Even though Vincent knew Anton's view of him, he also knew his own heart (and knew that his heart could never be taken to take flights of fancy) and so remained silent about his 'true calling.' Instead he absorbed all that Anton told him—then wrung from it that which did not fit him {or applied}…like a wet kitchen towel twisted between maidenstrong~sculleryhands.

Anton was blunt and expressed his frustration with Vincent, often:
his work was
> too rushed,
> too rough,
> too frantic.
That he needed to slow down, take time, 'finish!' He suggested that Vincent should, instead of concentrating his efforts solely on drawing, take up oil painting. Oil painting was what Anton did. Vincent admitted to Anton that nothing would please him more than to explore Color
> (the colors of Masters: Millet, Israëls, and even Ingres)
"But," Vincent affirmend, "It would not be right."
"Why on earth not!" Anton railed.
"Because," Vincent replied, "I'm not good enough yet."

Anton slapped Vincent's shoulder—hard. "You know more about Art than most painters. Hell, Boy, it's in your blood! Don't worry about such things."

Vincent would not be swayed. For it was not only the matter of not being good enough, it was a matter of money.

But after a few more weeks of Anton's force (and the giving of a small moneypurse), Vincent assented. Anton did, however, caution his wife's cousin, "Mind. Not all paints are the same. Especially now with them coming mixed…"

he trailed off, to reminisce,

a tangent about how when he'd learned from his
master to combine raw pigment…the sensation of
coming to the canvas with one's own elements…
but then he snapped
—almost visibly—
and his eyes looked a little wild, as if he (in his mental
detachment)
had forgotten Vincent's presence…

"…what was I saying?" he asked.
"About where I could buy good paints for less money."
"Oh yes. And when you see him, tell him I sent you."
It just so happened that Vincent had also received his
allowance from his father. So, with Anton's money and his
own, he bought canvases, paints, brushes, an easel, solvent
(and what other miscellaneous items the store owner could
"sell"—for the store owner was adept at spotting 'aspiring'
artists and masterful at hawking his wares).
Back at his studio (the shack) he opened the tubes of
color (having carefully selected a traditional Dutch palette).
At first he was frightened. What if he'd made a
mistake…messed it up. He was timid and frugal. He thinned
everything—to save the precious pigment. But then, as he felt
himself letting go there came upon him such a feeling of
freedom
(a feeling he'd never *ever* known)
that he found his new brushes gliding through the creamy,
buttery color
(sliding like Schiffs upon the Sea~ whispers like wind~
trees of home).
He breathed it in deep, that oily sweetnut smell, and there
—he praised God.
For he knew he'd found his vocation.
***

82

Meanwhile Pastor Theodorus waited,
        {with a strange letter in his hand}
for his son, Theo, to return home.
        He did not have to wait long. And when the young man
crossed his family's home's threshold, the patriarch swiftly and
mercilessly boxed his ear. "What is the meaning of this!" He
shook the letter in Theo's face.
"I can explain," Theo cried, holding his throbbing lobe.
        The father took the son by the arm and led him to the
church. What they were about to discuss was too damning to
be explored within the walls of their home
        —the outside was not safe either…
        Theodorus' wife was
                        about, somewhere, painting.

        For the pastor, there was only one safe haven. And,
after becoming safely tucked inside the small country parish's
closet-of-an-office, Theodorus continued his rant. "And to be
contacted like this! From a complete stranger! You think I
don't know how you conduct yourself in Paris!"
        Theo was, in fact, surprised. He'd really believed his
father ignorant of the life he led—so he played dumb…and coy.
"Now Father," he condescended, "I don't know what you're
talking about."
"Le Chat! That's what I'm talking about. As if I haven't worried
about you night and day…for your eternal soul! And then
there's this letter, from…this…Classina Hoornik addressing me
in familiar terms. Have you no sense? Can you not see that
she's after your inheritance! This, on top of all I've suffered
with your brother! My God, are you trying to kill me!"
        Theo had never seen his father riled so. He tried to
placate him, telling him that he had it all under control.
"Control. I don't want to hear it, Theo."
        The old man seemed to crumble. "I don't think I can
take much more."
        Theo put his hand on his father's arm. The man pulled it
away, as if his son's touch burnt. "Fix it. Fix it now, Theo."
At a loss, Theo asked, "How?"
        The pastor rubbed his temples.

And they were both quiet for a while.

"Did you know," Theodorus finally broke, "they're transferring me?"

"No, Father. Why?"

"Promotion, they say."

"More money?"

"A little. Hardly worth the trouble of moving—again. But it's worse. The town they're sending me to is predominantly...Catholic."

The two men heaved deep sighs. That fact was not easy for Protestants.

"Besides," Theodorus continued, "I am having troubles..."

Theo could see his father was struggling to confess.

"What is it, Father? Tell me. If I can help, I will."

"Well: it's...money."

"You said this was a promotion."

"And it is. It's just that I've been sending Vincent more...because he's down there all alone. And he's so committed—plus...I worry about him...there...with all that...sin. I wanted him to have what he wanted. I wanted to keep him busy—occupied—out of trouble's way. Besides, I've been paying Mauve to instruct him. And it's not been cheap, I tell you!"

The father couldn't have known, but with each profession of concern for his eldest son, his middle son's jealousy grew. Yet he listened. For as long as Theodorus worried about Vincent—he did not focus on Theo... or Theo's life in Paris or See.

But the father's confidence did end. That was when Theo touched brilliance, and said, "Let me send the money to Vincent."

"Oh no! I could never. Not after what happened between the two of you."

This, too, drove a nail through Theo's heart. Was he so foul? Was not his money even good enough for his brother?

But Theo was an expert at keeping on task. He countered.
"Fine. I'll send it to you. Vincent will never know."
     The pastor weighed the deceit knowing that ethics
weighed heavy…and that the price for their pound of flesh
     —{from a preacher's purse}—
cost such that he could not afford their morality.
***

There was a knock at the door. See jumped. Her mind immediately returned to the rape. She broke out in a cold sweat and her hands shook but she stood perfectly still...hoping that whoever it was would think the apartment empty—and leave.
More knocks came.
See's heart pounded so hard it came up into her throat, into her eardrums where she heard it thrumming like a train's engine—rhythmic and fierce.
More knocks—and then a note slipped
beneath the door. See could hear footsteps...a lady's
foots

t

e

ps...

diminish
ing.

When she was sure the deliverer had gone, See ran to the note and (with her one good eye—for the other was still swollen) she read:
"Miss Jo Bonger."
There came upon See a feeling she'd never felt so keen: jealousy. She ripped the letter open with her fingernails...but sank down onto Theo's couch when she read, "My Dearest Theo,"
It was as if someone had struck a fieryred branding iron into her heart: Theo was already engaged.
***

Vincent had brought his paints to Anton, who inspected them with an irritableness that worried Vincent. It had not been very long since Anton had suffered from an attack. His doctor said it was melancholia. Whatever it was, it put an end— temporarily—to Vincent's tutelage and had nearly cost the man his life

(something Vincent's cousin, Jet, relayed concerning a knife|>…and poison).

"I don't have to stay long," Vincent said to Anton. He could see that Anton was still not well.

"Don't be silly. I'm fine. Let's paint. It's the best thing for me."

But, as Vincent began setting his easel up (and getting his paints out) Anton grew more insistent that Vincent was doing everything wrong.

"Here," he nearly shouted, "Like this!"

And then, after Vincent had prepared his palette, more severe criticisms fell.

"Why the dark Dutch? Don't you know anything Vincent? Have you never heard of the Impressionists! That is old! Old! OLD! And I will not have it in my home do you understand me!"

Vincent stared, wide-eyed, but then applied more light colors—as he knew that was characteristic of the 'Impressionists.' He did not tell Anton that he felt such movements ridiculous because no one could ever do more for Art than Israëls and his kind: those who, in rich tradition, captured the plight of the downtrodden as brilliantly in "dark Dutch" as the novelists Eliot, Zola and Dumas had done in words.

The day progressed worse. They were painting a still life of fruit, plate, metal and linen. Vincent applied his thick creamy paint. Anton 'tsked' but remained, silent. Then Vincent removed his thick creamy paint—then used thinner.

"No no no! You're APPLYING paint. Not taking it away!"

Anton, literally, batted Vincent's drenched paintbrush away from his canvas. Vincent did not know what to do so he sat there, some time, doing nothing at all. But even this irritated Anton.

"Paint! You're here to paint. Do you think I need this practice? I don't need to be wasting my time if you're not serious about Art!"

"But I am," the words escaped before Vincent could hold them back.

Anton pointed his paintbrush at Vincent's canvas. Waiving it, insistently. So Vincent tried. But all he could see was that one spot, the spot he'd messed up—that was thick with wet paint…and there was only one way to continue on…he had to get that paint off. So he reached—trying to be as quick as he could—and with his fingers took a swipe.

Then Anton went mad.

He stood,

threw his canvas to the ground,

pointed to the door and screamed,

"Get out!"

Vincent, horrified, stammered something like, "I just had to…" but Anton's anger grew with each passing resistance to his command. He even broke his brush in two screaming at the top of his lungs: "Get out! Get out! Get out! I will not have a lunatic in my home. Which is the only kind of person who would use their fingers…to PAINT!"

Vincent scrambled to get his things together. He did not bother to cap his tubes of paint. As he was near-running out the door, his cousin Jet came to him: "Vincent, don't be mad." Vincent replies, "I'm not. I'm just sorry I've disturbed him so much. Please forgive me."

"Oh Vincent," she cried, "You can't know…" but Anton could be heard screaming in the background. Just before Jet closed the door her eyes locked with Vincent's and told all he needed to know.

Outside]—alone,

then and there,

he set his things on the ground

and went to his knees.

His hands folded,

he said aloud, "Dear God, please keep Jet safe. Please ease Anton's suffering. And let

them know that You love them."

He felt something hit his back. Some children, who'd been watching, were throwing stones and chanting, "Loon-a-tick…loon-a-tick…"

Vincent returned to praying, suffering Youth's assaults for a few minutes more (and secretly praying for their souls as well) before he rose, gathered his things, and began his long walk home.

***

When Theo arrived home in Paris, See was waiting. As the door lock yielded, she readied her aim. As Theo's head emerged, she flung the washbasin. It greatly missed him—shattering its porcelain against the wall.

"You bastard!" she yelled.

Before Theo had fully entered, he looked both ways down the halls. One door had opened. It was the nosey old woman who lived with many cats.

"Quiet!" he said to See.

But See

        (like the old lady's cats

        with the rats that came at night for crumbs)

had been waiting to lunge. Her claws caught his neck hard—he bled on his collar. He struck her back with all the fury he'd held in

        (from his time with his father).

She screamed he was killing her.

He screamed, "So what's new! I'm killing my own father—why not you!"

"You're the Devil!" she cried.

"You'll see," he spat out her name like venomacid, "See, just how evil I can be."

See held up Jo's letter. "I know…about your engagement." See tried to spit the same venomacid into her tone when she cried, "Sir. And you've badly abused me. Ruined me!" but the youngness in her, what had been so naïve, dissolved her (like acid) and she wept, uncontrollably…what am I to do?" she sobbed.

Theo, being moved by her suffering more than he'd expected to be, began the explanation of his plan (the one he'd hatched while watching the countryside pass—outside his train's window).

***

Vincent decided that the best thing to do was to write Anton and Jet a letter. That way, if Anton was still not well, it would not prove as taxing on him—as a visit.

The letter was filled with positivism, encouragement, and Art. He shared that he greatly admired Ingres' use of 'cad' (cadmium) red on his "Joan of Arc." He said that he wished them well and looked forward to the day they could see each other again. And when he posted it he hoped for a speedy reply.

He always hoped for speedy replies to his letters…and he wrote many. To his family—and to his friends: for his letters were as if letters written to himself. Letters he'd hoped someone would write to him: a word of cheer, a sharing of hope—a condolence when things were bad (though he always tried to keep his sufferings to himself).

However, whether letters came or not Vincent painted. And for this—this gift of oil—he would forever hold Anton Mauve, dear.

When a letter from Jet finally came in the post, Vincent (in spite of being terribly hungry), joyously thanked God—for Jet informed him that Anton was better (even though it was too early for him to come to their home). She wrote that she hoped his painting was going well and looked forward to the day they'd see each other again. Although secretly, and silently, he'd hoped Jet would have sent a little money with her letter, her words, her writing itself, raised his spirit and he determined that if he couldn't eat—he'd paint.

The fact was, Vincent had already spent all of Mauve's money (and his allowance) on paints and supplies. So every day he waited, anxiously, for the mail to come. Praying his father's letter, and money, would be there. Day-after-day he waited, weeks past what they had agreed upon.

He finally broke down and wrote to his father in desperation—that he would, within the next day, be without money for food. He did not tell him that he'd already been doing so for nearly a week.
***

When Pastor Theodorus received Vincent's letter he immediately went to the church. He'd learned not to read them at home—for his wife, with some sort of uncanny sense, would suddenly appear and demand to know what had become of her favorite son.

In his   closet[]office   he read Vincent's request. He'd already learned, from all of his son's past {zealousness}, that his boy was, most-likely, already starving. "Damn!" he swore.

For he had no money. And it was obvious that Theo, who'd promised his father that he'd send money as soon as he was paid, had not yet held up his part of the bargain.

The father racked his brain what to do. He could not let Vincent starve. So he did what many poor relatives did (if they could), he went to his much-richer, older brother (Vincent's godfather and namesake).

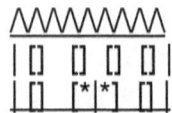

In a well-furnished, tastefully-rich home:

"It must not look like Charity," Pastor Theodorus cautioned, "for he will not accept that."
"Pride, dear brother." Elder Vincent smiled.

"Yes. I know. You never have approved of the choice I made, entering the clergy."

Elder Vincent poured himself a drink, but coughed into a burgundy-colored handkerchief (the wine color served to camouflage the tiny blood droplets he'd been recently finding in his kerchiefs after such coughing fits), "You were always Mother's favorite because of it."

Pastor Theodorus remained reverentially silent.
"And me," the elder brother continued, "she detested because I made my fortune in business. The 'Money Changer' I think she

called me from her deathbed. With her next breath she called for you to pray for her. It was one of her last…

…how ironic now that it's your son—my namesake, Vincent—who is in need of what your 'expensive' spirituality can't afford."

"Yes, Brother."

It was the most difficult thing Pastor Theodorus had ever done—humbling himself before his older brother that way. And his older brother savored every moment of it.

"So be it," Elder Vincent waived his hand, "I'll go see him in, did you say, the Hague?"
"Yes."
"Where he worked for me? Oh yes. Now I remember—it wasn't *good* enough for him."

Theodorus wanted to defend. He wanted to tell his brother that Vincent had sensed a higher calling. But he knew that if he deprived him of the pleasure of his lording, then Vincent would starve. So he simply replied, "Yes."
"Well. I'll go there under the pretense of Goupil. And see just what **MY** godson is up to. Then I'll offer to pay him for whatever nonsense he's doing. Is that deceitful enough to protect…"

Elder Vincent
        latched onto every syllable
                    as if Venus Nipples,
"…your son's delicate sensibilities?"

"Yes, Vincent. Thank you."

Theodorus rose, leaving behind him a magnificent estate, vast gardens, and a brother who'd finally managed to purchase his one desire.
***

Theo worked hard to get See calmed. He wondered how a woman could get so worked up. That's when she told him about the blood...and about Andres.

She expected Theo to rush away from her, seek out his friend and defend her honor. Theo, however, had more pressing business at hand. He told her about his family. How his older brother had been the one to go into the art business before him...but had got 'religion.' How their father, in spite of his condemnation of his eldest son's zealousness, seemed to prefer Vincent to him.

When See asked how that made any difference to what was happening between them, |she—him|, he paced the room.

"My Uncle Cent is very rich, and is very ill. The doctors predict he won't last through the year."

"So." See said.

"This means that, with Vincent out of the way, I stand to inherit a good deal."

"What are you saying?"

He went to her side, assuming the epitome of charm.

"I'm saying that if Vincent, who's obviously crazy—you should have SEEN him with those dirty miners! Anyway, if Vincent were to be found insane—and institutionalized...I would control his inheritance."

"What does that matter?" See cried.

He clutched her hands in his. "Don't you understand? With money comes freedom."

Then cruelty came.

"And you. You don't really have a choice do you?"

"What do you mean?"

"Do you even know how to keep yourself from 'getting with child'?"

That cut struck her deep.

Theo drank in the moment...waiting for her silent acquiescence.

Her shoulders confirmed it.

So he became—all warmth and comfort.

He wrapped his arms around her as if a duvet.

He pulled her head to his chest, stroked her jetblack hair,

kissed her swollen face.

94

"Did I hurt you...badly," he asked.

She rubbed her arm. "No."

She lied.

"That's good," he replied. "I don't want to hurt you, See."

He kissed her split lip. "I love you. I want you to marry me."

She wanted to protest, to ask about 'Jo,' but his tenderness felt good and his voice a soothing balm to her fears—

the fears she'd been living with alone...since he'd left her.

"So," Theo said, "the truth is that you can't know...if you are with child...or who the father is. Andres? Me? But I have a plan."

See's eyes grew dim.

She saw,

through his voice,

her doom.

And they both would know—within weeks time—whether seed had been sown to her womb.

***

Vincent was shocked to receive a letter from his Uncle Cent announcing a pending visitation to Vincent's studio after his attendance to other business in the Hague.

Vincent immediately made haste to put the place in order. He gathered his paint tubes into a box (though some had already lost their tops). He attempted to line up his painted canvases in such a way as to display them. He picked up the wadded letters {early revisions of what had already been sent} and tossed them into the pot-bellied stove's just-barely burning coal. He was, he thought, fortunate enough not to have any food to clean up and his pipe had long since been empty.

When Uncle Cent arrived at Vincent's 'studio' he began, immediately, condemning its lack of 'substance.' The walls, themselves, bared cracks such that the outside world showed between them. He did not remove his coat and abruptly came to business. "I want to see if there is anything of your work that I'd like to buy."

Vincent's eyes beamed with joy. It was more than a great compliment that his Uncle Cent—being in such great esteem in the art business—might find something of value in his work. So he scurried

(a starving little mouse)

to show

{excitedly}

all of the paintings he'd done, but Uncle Cent was reluctant— for most of them were still wet...as they'd been painted so thickly...that even the oldest of the stretches promised to get the rich man's clothes dirty.

So Vincent decided (while making great efforts not to touch his Uncle—for fear of getting paint on him) to show Elder Vincent his drawings.

These, the uncle quickly thumbed through and then said, "Fine. I'll take these. And if you can do more—with much-improved quality—I will purchase those as well."

Elder Vincent gave his godson a purse but when Vincent tried to hand him his drawings he said, tersely, "No. Send them by post." The man had managed not to allow a single of his fingers to touch his nephew's.

Vincent watched the carriage carry the man away that had, throughout his life, seemed so distant and prayed, "Thank You God. Thank You!"

***

There was no denying it. See was pregnant. Her 'time' had not come and she was sick (not just in the mornings but all of the day) and more miserable because Theo never let her, for one moment, believe he'd have anything to do with the baby.

It was all part of the plan.

See meant absolutely nothing to Theo, with regard to the way he lived his life in Paris. It was as if See had never existed, for after work at Goupil Theo would meet Andres at Le Chat, where he'd stay until all hours of the night.

When he came home to his apartment (which was infrequent) he usually smelled of absinthe and whores. He'd take particular effort, in cleaning himself, to make sure See knew what he'd been up to.

See was not yet showing (it had only been a month past her 'time') but her desperation was tangible...to Theo.

Still...he waited.
Pushing>...
Abandoning>...
pushing>...
waiting...

until he nearly felt afraid for his life when he slept. That's when he knew she was ready. So he took her to Le Chat.

Salis, however glad he was to see Theo, could not disguise his displeasure at seeing See. It was his policy: once a girl was gone|she was dead. But Theo was that good of a customer—for Theo, he made an exception.
"Would you like your regular, Messer van Gogh?"
"Yes. And one for the lady as well."

See was about to protest, for even though she did not want to be pregnant she knew absinthe to be poison—on many levels—and did not want such a fate for the life within her. But Theo insisted. And Salis agreed, even though he cursed under his breath something to the effect, "Lady my..."

With clouds in front of them Theo raised his glass.
"To the future."

See cried.
"Not here," Theo reprimanded, "Or I swear I'll leave you on the street."

She stopped herself.

"Now drink."

 See put the glass to her lips, trying only to take a little bit, but Theo pushed the glass' bottom up so that the milky liquid ran down her throat, down her chin and the front of her dress—See did not flinch. She knew her messed dress was the least of her worries.

"So. See. Vincent. If he's insane then I'll be rich."

"But you already have plenty of money."

"My dear," he cooed, "What good is money when I will not be allowed to marry the love of my life

 ...the mother of my child?" <he pulled.

 It was first time Theo had ever said that the life in her belly was his. The admission was a promise: in her eyes. One she desperately needed, for somehow her parents had found out that she was with child—

(by a father, unknown)

—and living as a whore...and they'd not only disinherited her (from what little money they had) but utterly disowned her in a letter that told her that she should consider them dead in her eyes.

 She did not know: Theo could write such things.

Her only salvation, and that of her unborn child's, was for Theo to marry her. It would solve everything.

"So, See..."

 She hated when he said that.

"...here's the plan..."

 He laid it out, on that table at Le Chat Noir, while never taking his eyes off the newest blonde who'd come to work the stage. Rumor had it she was Norwegian. Theo had always liked Scandinavia.

"I won't. I can't! I couldn't bear it."

"Just think of it like this: that selfless act will ensure us being together."

"But...it makes me sick just to think of it."

 The blonde thrust her breasts. Theo's eyes twinkled.

He took a sip.

"I know, I know" his mouth said,
        —like a puppet's wood with a controllingman behind it—
"but he is my brother. It's not like a stranger. And no one else
will ever know."
"But I don't want to."
        He slapped her so hard that her ears rung and her skin
stung. Salis, seeing this, was making his way to Theo's table
(for not even his best customers could rough up women—
inside the bar) but he didn't have to traverse far. Theo knew—
oh how he knew—the rules. He grabbed See's arm, hard, and
pulled her out of Le Chat.
        In the street he screamed at her, loud enough for
everyone to hear her humiliation, "You Whore! There is nothing
else. Do you understand me!"
        She fainted. It may have been the absinthe—or the fact
she'd not been able to eat without throwing up and had grown
quite skinny. Theo carried her to the apartment and laid her
atop the bed.   She tried to stay unconscious for as long
as she could—praying she were dead—for, in sleep, it was the
only time she knew peace…since she'd met Theo. But her
eyes fluttered.
        He knew she was faking it. So he slapped her again.
"Don't try to fool me! Don't you ever try to fool me," he
screamed and acted as if he were going to strike her, over and
over but stopped…mid-swing…acting|exercising a great deal of
self-discipline not to hurt her.

        He paused—for effect.

"So, See…let me make this simple. Vincent falls in love with
you—which he will, because he's never been with a woman
and you'll do a good job making him fall in love with you. You
tell him this sob story about how you got into trouble and you
don't want to be a whore…but you have no choice. You tell
him that if he marries you that you'll stop being a prostitute.
He'll eat that up. I know my brother."
"But…" See stammered.
"No buts. You do this and I'll marry you."
"But…how does me getting your brother to propose to me
make him insane?"

"Don't you worry. I'll take care of that."

"What about my family?"

"After we're married, they'll take you back. I'm sure of it.
Besides, if they don't—initially—they will. I hear they're hurting
real bad for money. If you make a 'good match' and can
promise them an annual salary—I'm sure they'll find their way
to 'forgiving' you."

Theo always did his legwork. It was true. When See
had left home it was in order to work and send money back to
her parents because cotton prices had fluctuated and were in a
downturn. She did not know, unlike Theo, that in fact—her
father's mill had burnt to the ground.

***

Vincent received the letter from his father. Just seeing the return address struck good cheer into his heart. For although his Uncle Cent (Elder Vincent) had purchased some of his drawings, he had not replied or responded to the many others Vincent had mailed to him. Nor had he sent additional monies. And Vincent's money was, as usual, nearly gone. But Vincent's good feelings about his father's letter did not live past the first sentences that read:

Dearest Vincent,

I regret to inform you that I will no longer be able to send you an allowance. However, your brother has been kind enough to assume what I no longer can. Please find enclosed…

It devastated him. Not only was he now dependent upon the very brother who'd betrayed him, but he now also knew that his own parents' financial situation had greatly worsened. He wrote, immediately, to his father…and to Theo. It was the first time, since the Borinage, that his hand formed his brother's name in ink:

Dear Theo,
Let me thank you for the enclosed amount…

***

See waited for the man she knew only from a single photograph. Waited for him whom Theo had described...there, where Theo swore they'd meet. Only Theo hadn't told her that the same street was filled with
—after dark (as with cockroaches)—
streetwalkers.

And these women were nothing like those at Le Chat: these were truly desperate women with missing teeth, sores about their mouths, and feet grown fat and swollen from hours of standing in the elements.

These were hard women and they did not like seeing a new woman—one softer than they were—for it seemed the men always went for the soft girls...and that meant the hard girls didn't eat. One, literally, chased See from the streetside—kicking at See's backside as she ran.

But what was she to do? She had to find Vincent and he had to believe she was one of them...and she was told to wait there...so she did the only thing she could...she fought the woman. She pulled her hair, bit her arm. The woman screamed and punched See in the stomach but See didn't have time to worry about her baby—suddenly there came a hand, two hands, and a man. She just made out red...
"Stop. There's no need for violence," he said.

The streetwalker didn't miss a beat. "Want some honey, Mister?" and adjusted her breast, which had shifted left.
"No. No, thank you." he replied. The streetwalker smiled.
"Hey Girls, we got a tender one here."

They all knew what that meant.

Vincent reached down to help See up. She saw that he didn't seem to actually look at her...or anyone. As if, by not seeing, he was able to help streetwalkers just the same as if they were the King himself. And See, keenly, felt the falsity of this. She'd learned from Theo. She knew that the only way he'd be able to see her—to want her—was to see the world he'd be pulling her up from...so she slapped his face.

And when he reeled, surprised at that reception, she slapped him again with all her strength.

"Hey," the streetwalker yelled, "what the hell do you think you're doin'!"

See watched what had thus shielded him—his veil of impartiality—fall. He took in the streetwalkers (all of them) and every ounce of their pain. He witnessed the darkness of their streetworld…and then he looked at See:
with her jetblack hair
and cowbrown eyes
and swore he'd never seen anything as beautiful…
…but she was…a…prostitute…and he couldn't…
See seized her moment,
grabbed his shoulder
and pulled his ear to her lips, "Help me."
He couldn't resist.

As they walked towards his studio the streetwalkers hissed, "Damn those soft women!"
***

Things couldn't have been going better, for Theo. He'd made some significant sales

(thanks to Miss Jo Bonger)

and held an air of promise for more profit. So that when he approached young Etiene Boussod

(son of Leon—who was a partner of Goupil—who'd had a sister who'd had a daughter who then married the son of Leon. Boussod's name stood alongside Goupil's, "Goupil—Boussod et Valadon" –though always in title…never tongue)

about purchasing art from the new Impressionists—

(promising that he, Theo, had close relationships with the samesaid artists thereby could acquire very good art… "Important Art"… "one day Expensive art" for next to nothing)

it was a symbol of power to ascent.

History:

It was no secret. Being Adolphe Goupil's real successor, Leon Boussod had, effectively, become one of the most influential men in European Art.

It is often the sad case: a father builds an empire and in spite of there being many heirs—not one desires to take his place. Thus was the case of the Goupil Empire. None of Adolphe's sons wanted their father's business (income…that was a different story) and only one, Albert, had even a glint of care for art (though his came from wanting to create art himself…but finding he hadn't the aptitude—so resigning himself—then collected trophies from those who could).

Through Etienne Boussod, Theo found a compatriot's ear (and expense account with full freedom to purchase—at his will…and discretion).

There would be more mergers, more associations, more purchases…but that made little impact on Theo's life—at that time…in Paris. For his Uncle Cent had long since secured Theo's inheritance (having earlier realized his investments) …and everything seemed to be going just as he'd planned.
***

They had only just arrived at Vincent's 'studio'
      (to which See responded with utter shock at the stark
      contrast between what Theo had conjured up to describe
      the brother—his extravagant, expensive life—and the
      reality of what stood before her)
when there came a knock. It was Jet Mauve, Anton's wife, and
she was visibly upset.

      Her mood did not much improve when she saw a woman
in Vincent's place {dressed in clothes that plied a specific
trade}. Still, she waited for proper address, which Vincent
(however willing to do) was unable to make. For the fact was,
he had not bothered to ask what the girl's name was that he'd
rescued from the street.

      The silence of appropriateness surmounted until Jet
could stand it no more, for the urgent matter that had brought
her to Vincent necessitated a more rapid progression: "My
name is Mm. Jet Mauve," she introduced herself.
"I am Se…" See's body automatically genuflected but she
caught herself before revealing her true name, "…in."

      Jet responded in polite kind, for in spite of her first
impression—based upon her dress and the lateness of hour,
not to mention the neighborhood itself—her manners struck her
fine.
"Sien, like the river?"
"Uh," See replied, "yes…Ma'am."
"Fine. Good."

      Jet turned to Vincent who stared, wide-eyed, at the girl
he'd thought he'd rescued but wondered, then, just who she
was…for he
      (with his eagle-like eyes of acuity)
surmised from her a refinery…could she not be…
      could she be…
from the streets? Yet he'd seen her there, fighting.

      And while he was wrestling such thoughts in his head
Jet's urgency grew such that she touched his arm.
"Vincent, I must speak with you!" she said
"What is it dear cousin?"
"It's Anton. He's bad."

      Vincent looked at the woman, then back to his cousin.
He felt, strangely, responsible for both. But felt himself pulling

to the one he didn't know, ushering her to a chair where, he noticed, a certain twist to her hip as she sat—there was no mistake what that meant.

"This poor girl," he thought.

Jet stamped the floor. Vincent turned to her.

"I will quickly build a fire and then we'll go."

See was amazed at his kindness, for before he left her there he said, "I have no money. There is little food but what there is of it…it's yours."

His eyes lingered, a moment, on her stomach. And with that…he, and the woman—his cousin—were gone.

***

"Listen Theo, I need the money."

"Everybody needs money Paul."

"I know, but my son. He's hurt. He needs medicine and it's expensive. And I'm here! Damn that I ever became…"

"Now don't get all worked up. Here," Theo motioned to Salis—who sent over one of his new German finds—"Drink up. The night's young. I'll make sure things are fine. Don't I always?"

Paul looked at Theo's eyes. They were eyes like a mirror to the heart of man where bones crushed against stone and flesh fed flesh. It was a mirror of himself—one that slivered into ever-increasing shards with every glass that emptied down their throats from the absinthe-abstracted sculpture growing out from the middle of the table.

Paul cried out, sometime that night, with genuine enthusiasm, "If I could but sculpt this…my family…"

Theo stayed until it would have otherwise proven unwise—in the morning he had to work at Goupil. But, this was work too—for at Le Chat, while collecting monies for Goupil's 'upstairs'

—meaning the art of his friends

and getting paid his wages for procuring such art he was also

—unbeknownst to Goupil—

collecting fees from his friends (the artists)

—as he'd, secretly, become many of his artist/friend's agent.

And Salis got a little bit of the cut, giving Theo a discount (based on volume) proving Le Chat fertile ground for Theo's business platform, where he found that his list of clients grew in exponentials:

to bottles (of various contents)

and bread

and cheese

and rents to be paid

and children to be fed

and women to be had—all of which Theo exacted, yet more, fees.

***

Inside Mauve's studio Vincent found Anton in front of two paintings. Both were like none he'd ever seen before. They were certainly not Mauve's style—nor of any living thing—Vincent swore. In fact, they'd been painted with such haste, such possession and fervor, that they literally dripped to the floor: as if God Himself, being so offended, were wiping them clean—with tears of solvent""'"

And then there was Anton. The horror of the sight of him! Standing there, eyes wide with craze,

brushes thrust between each finger on his right hand and tubes of paint in his left—and his face!
Paint oozed from the corners of his mouth.

Vincent gasped. Anton turned to him, throwing his instruments to the ground. Throwing himself on the man he'd sworn would never set foot in his house again. "Vincent! You came! Thank you thank you thank you."

Anton, with his arms thrust around Vincent's neck, was smothering him in paint...but Vincent didn't mind. He was used to the lost...and the price one paid for being there...in their terror. "What is it Anton?" Vincent, softly, asked.

When he finally got Anton settled, what then began was a tale—one that would change Vincent's life—forever.
***

With cash in hand (and stashed) Theo became 'the man' at Le Chat, at least with respect to the artists.

Before—many of the artists at Le Chat had known that Theo worked for Goupil. That was not new news. However, after Theo's arrangement with Etienne Boussad—
to purchase 'fine,' 'modern,'—
became known
(due to the efforts of Theo himself)
it seemed *every* artist wanted to befriend him.

But those who were serious about their Art wouldn't stoop to 'groveling.' Besides anyone who'd lived much in the art world knew—salesman couldn't influence squat. It was the buyers! They bought. And with Boussad's blessings on Theo to buy—Theo found that his table was almost always filled round with artists of varying shapes, sizes, colors—aesthetics, (experience).

Oh! The debates were glorious!

Almost as great as Salis' ecstasy {for while Theo was at the table...he kept the tableround in absinthes (and experience)}.

Andres was right there too. In fact, although he kept his own apartment, it was mere formality. He and Theo were living together. And, they'd acquired a new taste—in their women—a sort of taste a bit here...there...a smorgasbord of flesh. All freshly supplied by Salis' ever-increasing stream...like farm-raised fish...of young and younger women.

You can just imagine, then, how well-received was a knock on the door:
(in the wee hours of the night...
just when passions were peaking
within the writhing den of slithering bodies)

from See, showing pregnant,
staring...wide-eyed...at that scene.
***

"I knew her, Vincent," Anton continued. "I was studying under..."

He went on to say he'd been studying under a Master, he and others that the Master had selected, when he was out
—in plen aire—
painting. She came to him asking if he'd like to spend some time with her.

"It began with just painting, though I knew what kind of girl she was. Those kinds of girls," he said.

Then staring straight into Vincent's eyes, "I was sure..."

Anton drifted off into a sort of jibbering reminiscence. Vincent saw that Jet was keeping herself hid, but present, and motioned her near. "How long has he been like this?" he asked.

"It began just after we went to bed...we'd..."

She grew visibly awkward.

"That's alright. I understand."

Anton looked to where Jet stood but his eyes saw nothing except what passed before them in his memory.

"Did he take anything? Drink? Medicines?"

She held up a vial. "These."

"What is it?"

"The doctor said it was for his heart, digitalis, I think. From the foxglove flower. Surely it wouldn't do this?"

Vincent looked at the white. "Surely not."

Then he sighed. For secretly he was hoping it was merely the poisoning of Physic, not the mind—or worse...Spirit.

He told Jet to leave.

To not look back and not to listen.

It was important she obey, no matter what she heard—even if he screamed—or wailed...

(for Vincent knew when troubled hearts first let loose,
their pain was no less destructive than a dyke—
overcome by a sudden rush of Spring's rain—flooding...,
they demolished all what dread fears not).

Jet, hesitatingly, agreed. Even though she knew (having been told by her uncle) that Vincent was not well himself, there was about him a great spirituality.

And she knew her husband
—this was not the first time—
and she knew that if Vincent failed, there was nothing left to
him…but insanity.

In the quiet.
"Anton."
The man stared at his paintings.
"Anton. Can you hear me?"
He did not break his stare but replied, "Is she gone?"
"Yes. It's just me…and God."
"God? God! He can't help me now! I'm doomed don't you
see!"
Anton took Vincent by the collar and shook him violently.
"Doomed to Hell!"
"Yes."
This was not…even in his fit of madness…what Anton
expected. It jolted him. "What do you mean by that? You're
supposed to be helping me!"
"I am."
"By telling me I'm going to Hell? That's helping me!"
"Yes."
There was something about his calm reserve. The fact
that this man, whom he'd been told could be quite violent
(by his wife's other cousin)
was sitting, amidst his physicality:
his raging,
his paintings,
his utter desperation…like some sort of stony monk.
"Are you flesh?" Anton stood, throwing his arms above his
head.
"Oh yes, Brother. I am just as much flesh as you are."
"Then how can you sit there like this?"
"Because I am here to help you…and…because you asked."
"I did?"
"Yes. Jet told me that you cried out my name over and over
again."
"She's crazy!"

Vincent laughed.

112

This, too, Anton did not expect. So he laughed, though not really knowing why...and so tried to cover it with further rant, but quickly afterwards—being spent—sat down.

And there they sat...
without saying one word...

for a long   long   time.
***

"What in the Hell are you doing here? You're supposed to be in the Hague!"

See sputtered, "I just can't, Theo. I just can't!"

The girls, and Andres made no attempt to cover themselves on the bed. In fact, they continued on—for none of them, perhaps except Theo, were anchored to that place...that room...their bodies:

they were somewhere, lost in their pleasures...

unbound by their skin.

Theo pulled See inside and slammed the door. "You're going to ruin everything."

"I just can't do it."

"You found him didn't you?"

"Yes. I did what you said."

"So what's the problem, See?"

She hesitated.

He slapped her.

One of the girls moaned.

Andres slapped another girl's thigh.

See cried.

Theo threw himself down on the couch, still naked, filled with disgust. "A simple thing. I ask you to do a simple thing and you can't even..." but before he could finish saying what he was saying, something had changed—

he'd not seen it coming—

See's hand stung his face: "How could you!" She lunged for the door. Theo lunged at her. Grabbing her waist

—feeling her rockhard belly—

but pulling her to the floor anyway.

The thud, he'd hoped...

"You stupid! You stupid..." then he kissed her mouth.

She wanted to fight back, to bite back, to keep him from her—but he was her child's father...she just knew...though he wasn't sure

and she couldn't prove it...

and there was still that part of her that dreamt
it was all a bad dream: that she'd wake to find him
beside her, her husband, a child, a wedding...

...the women gathered their things from the floor.

Some of them watched See out of the corners of their eyes. They were the ones who'd had experience with wives.

Yet, See had been successfully tamed. For while he made love to her he whispered those things
（those things she so wanted to hear)
and made promises
（those women were not his but Andres…who needed a place to stay)
and gave her body pleasure, that night, that she'd never known before.
***

"Did you love her," Vincent asked.

"Yes. I think…I don't know."

Anton rubbed his oily hands through his hair, staining it yellow and red and blue. "When she told me she was pregnant I didn't know what to do. I asked my friends and they told me it was the oldest trick in the book. That the whores knew that artists came from families that could afford to have artists in the family."

Vincent smiled.

"Yeah, funny huh?" Anton smiled, "Well how was I supposed to know? So they said that the girls say they're pregnant, even when they're not, just to get you to marry them. And so I…"

"You?"

"…so I told her that I would…never marry a girl like her…and…"

Vincent watched his eyes begin to shift—like a fish on a line that's gone just as far as it can—before fighting…"Stay with me, Anton. I know it's hard. But God must break down what He will build back up. And you must *LET* Him…or the pain will never *NEVER* stop."

Yet, when Anton turned his eyes to Vincent's
      (eyes pleading like a sick child riddled with the pain of
      fever and begging its parent to fix it),
it took everything in Vincent's power to keep himself still
      (like an angler…waiting…letting the fight go on…fighting
      the urge to pull…without tremor or flinch…waiting…)
"…and then she…"

"Yes, Brother. Yes, she what?"

"…she…"

"I'm here for you…"
      (…it was almost time to snap the wrist…)
"…she drowned herself…"
      (snap)
"God forgives…"
      (but he was too quick)

"But," Anton interrupted, "that wasn't it."

Vincent accidentally sucked air in, for having been too hasty. It had been a while since he'd ministered. "I'm sorry, Anton."

"For what?"

"For interrupting you."

This, further, pulled Anton away from the moment. Vincent could feel his retreat. Inside he was screaming at himself condemnations for failing to be God's witness...for failing to...listen...instead of feeding his vanity—to speak...and yet he knew, God was working there—in that room with him— and so he stopped trying to be...and became.

"Okay Anton. I'm going now."

"But you can't leave."

"You want me to leave. I can sense it."

"Yes. I do. But I don't. I know. I don't make sense. It's just so hard. I...just can't...take it anymore...Vincent!"

Vincent put his arm around Anton. "You don't have to tell me. I don't matter."

"But you were a minister and I can't tell anyone else." Anton's shoulders shivered, he was crying.

"You can tell God. After all, my dear Anton," Vincent lifted Anton's eyes to his own, "He's the only One who can save you...from yourself."

So Vincent rose to leave but before he did Anton fell to his knees, before his paintings, scraping them away into a pile of browngrey and cried out... "...she *was* pregnant."
***

Pastor Theodorus and his family packed up their belongings and moved, once again, to a new parish. It was not an easy move. Theodorus had liked where he'd been—and, if truth were told, he found that growing older meant he liked (and was capable of) moving less. And when he was feeling in a particularly persecuted mood, he swore that the Diocese was participating in the (not uncommon) practice of keeping one's undesirables (be them enemies or simply fat from the lean) on the move…until they dropped dead…from fatigue…or sorrow.

Always with the promise of a little bit more money, a little bit larger parish-office; it amazed him what a man would do for a bit of metal…or a ribbon…or the sash of a girl's skirt.
***

After everyone had left, leaving but moments for him to clean and dress for work, Theo addressed See: "You must go back. There is no other choice. Right now my brother is actually making some progress with his art. My parents are supporting him. How? I don't know. Father had made arrangements with me to send him money—which I haven't—but then my brother sends me these!"

Theo pointed to a thickness of canvases stacked against the wall.
"And my father is down my neck about keeping up commitments..."

See laughed. Theo sneered.
"Oh shut up. So you can see. This is not going to plan. If my brother actually becomes an artist, which I highly doubt—he's too religious to be a true artist—but that's beside the point...if he actually becomes an artist, his work will be mediocre at best."

See went to the stack. Theo heard the wooden frames gently crack against each other.
"You see what I mean? What am I saying! You can't know what I mean. You're just a stupid whore who wouldn't know art if it..."
"My father collected art."
"Well," Theo turned to her, straightening his tie, "Isn't that ironic then."
"Yes. It is."

See held one of a woman, bent at the waist. A working woman. She began to cry.
"Oh not that again, my God, is that all you do!"

She thought, "I think the sentiment in this is good," but said nothing.
"So as I was saying. I'll get stuck supporting another no good mediocre artist—as if I don't have enough of them leeching off me now. I need Vincent put away. So I can get that inheritance. Do you hear me?"

See was still staring at the painting.
"Do you hear me?"
{she heard him say}
just before he boxed her left ear.
***

119

When Vincent got back to his studio the fire had gone
out and the woman, Sien, was gone. That did not surprise
him...and yet something about the woman haunted him. He
sat, in those wee hours (for it was growing dawn), and sketched
her:
> a mysterious woman in black...
> a dark beauty with dark eyes...
> with a secret hidden...and filled with sorrow...

while outside, amongst the cornfields, the crows filled their
gullets with what could be found...
> —on the ground, within gourds—
...those seeds what were sown in fertile grounds
and tilled
and disked with human sweat...and blood.
***

Theo sent a message to Goupil's. A family situation had come up and he would be late. They'd come to expect it. Not only because it happened rather more frequently but because they'd had
(as a company)
experience with the van Gogh family. They knew that *certain* members had *certain* temperaments and, as a result, had *special* (*extra*) needs.

However, the young man, Theo, had proven himself exceedingly good. And by 'good' (from Goupil's point of view) meant bringing in nice profits.

At the train station Theo repeated See's assignment. She assured him that she understood what she was supposed to do. He told her there was nothing else for her. If she showed up in Paris again, having failed him, he'd treat her as if he'd never known her.
"If you fail again, you'd be better off," he whispered in her ear, "to throw yourself into the…"
he hesitated,
"Sien? That's what you came up with for a name for yourself?"
Then he laughed at her. It was a cold gesture. It reminded her of the glass, which had—by then—separated them [each] from the other.
***

Vincent's daily life carried on normally.
He saw a scene,
felt the scene,
longed to make the scene that which would elevate God's Art to
the world...
but failed.

Always failing. He threw his paints into their box with
disgust. Frustrated that he would never have the skill he strove
for.

He bit a crust of bread. Never forgetting that fasting was
the key to moving mountains. Then spit it out onto the ground
knowing that the crows would, later, enjoy the luxury.

He lifted the wineskin to his lips, but not before praying
that the blood of Christ would course through his body, make
him whole, forgive his sins—
listing
all
those
things
he'd done
(and failed to do)
and then...feeling sure of God's grace...sipped but a little.

In solemnity, he returned to his canvas. Praising God for
all the beauty He'd created, for saving a sinner like him, for
giving him his purpose...and gifts...and for saving Anton.
It was near dark, having eaten nothing—
(for the crust was all he'd had...and he figured the birds
needed it at least as much)
—he felt as if his every step
each
and
every one of them
contained Bunyan's entire mountainside/^\.
He longed to collapse. To sleep.
He felt he could hardly carry...on...and
when he entered his studio,
he found...Sien...then fell, involuntarily, into the blackness of
non-dreaming.
***

122

The plans were made: Theo was to travel with Andres to the Bonger family estate.

It was a grand estate.

Theo

(being raised with his family's sensibilities regarding the trades)

had always assumed an air of superiority over Andres and Jo

(even though he never scorned their money).

For in the pecking order of things it was:

the clergy (however poor)

that ranked between

the established 'rich' (though often cash-poor)

and the working rich

<to whom the poor rich looked down their noses on>.

Theo, however, was proving himself more cosmopolitan than class conflict. He cared nothing about status...it was all about money. And Andres' and Jo's family had plenty of it.

Theo was shown to his room. It was (though he'd have never admitted it) the nicest room he'd ever been in second only to his Uncle Cent's (as rich as the Bonger family was...they held no contest with Elder Vincent).

Introductions were made shortly before dinner

(a 21-course affair including:

freshly-killed elk,

freshly-caught salmon,

quail's eggs and

a champagne soufflé—amongst the other foods

and multitudinous bottles of fine wines).

Theo found Jo's father to be superbly intelligent about business and her mother proved the model of grace (though he did wonder how it was the mother could have such fine features...while the daughter had inherited such less 'face').

After the women excused themselves

(requiring an hour to undo the hour it took to dress)

the men drank stronger spirits and smoked and made the required arrangements.

It was

—to all concerned, and after that evening's formal interview—

a fine match.

In the morning Theo was taken hunting. Everything was going quite good. Messr Bonger shot a 12-point buck. It should have been a celebration of manhood. A bonding of brothers-in-arms. A sporting event filled with good cheer, but Theo came quite unglued.

He'd never seen anything shot to death before. In fact, being a preacher's son, he'd never even hunted. Everything they'd ever eaten came from someone else's slaughter. So while the other men

(Andres, his father and some others who'd come for the hunt)

left the servants to gather and care for the game while they drank to their victory, Theo slipped away…

…kneeling beside the elk, he saw that it was still breathing. Messr Bonger had hit in low—in the gut…and something green oozed…and it stank…

Theo covered his nose. A servant told him he shouldn't be there.

"What is that awful smell?" Theo asked.

"It's from his liver."

"What is that?"

"Beats me. I just know, when they hit them there—the poor bastard—it hurts and takes a long time for them to die."

…the beast panted…

"How do you know it hurts them?" Theo asked, before turning away.

"Look at his eyes. They say it all."

Then the servant killed the beast.

***

When Vincent awoke he wondered if he'd imagined the woman, but found her still there.

At first, being alone with Vincent was awkward for See. It was strange to be called by what she'd created herself to be
        —a river that existed and swelled and consumed…a lie.

They existed, quietly, for a time.
It took her time to engulf it enough
        —like biting off parts of a large play—
to suspend her belief in her unique being…to automatically respond to
(thus becoming)
 Sien.
"Would you like something to eat, Sien," he politely asked.
        She knew, from when they met before that there'd be
        nothing to eat.
"No thank you," she replied, "I'm not hungry."
        Vincent knew those kinds of lies. "Here," he said, "Have
a little wine to drink then. It will strengthen your spirits."
        Sien did not refuse this.
        Vincent watched her drink it deep and wondered
whether she was a Christian but was experienced enough to
know it was too early to ask.
"I have to go and paint. I'll be gone all day—maybe late into
the evening. Will you be alright here by yourself?"
        She was not accustomed to someone caring for her
wellbeing. It startled her. So she said nothing.
        Vincent wondered if he'd assumed too much. If she'd
simply returned for a warm place—a few moments respite—or
a potential customer…so he acknowledged this. "I don't want
to encourage you," Vincent said, softly, adding the last bit of
coal he had to the fire (which was so little that it could but give
an allusion to warmth).
        Sien remained. Vincent stood to leave. His easel
gathered, paints, canvas. Looking outside was unnecessary—
he could feel the wind through the drafty wood walls.
        Sien saw him hesitate. "Does it bother you?"

Vincent shook his head. He knew she meant the wind. "You can stay," he replied, "as long as you wish. You have no obligation to me and I will not partake in your services."

He turned his piercing eyes to hers. It was the first time she saw that he and Theo could actually be...brothers.
***

The new parish office was much more grand—if for
nothing else but the fact that emptiness echoed throughout the
chapel:
only the graveyard was near-filled that Sunday service when
Pastor Theodorus
        (while expounding on the epistles of Paul)
wondered what he'd done to deserve such banishment…into
the wild…deserted and without a flock of Protestants…while
the hungry Catholic wolf pack gathered under their
well-adorned spires…waiting for the old prey to tremble…to
loose his footing…to fall behind the safety of his herd
and become their feast.
***

Vincent had learnt, from earlier ventures painting outside
(on windy days) that one must be adequately anchored
          —otherwise that which one creates is vulnerable to
falling victim to what moves beyond (unseen yet felt).
Vincent was always leery of the unseen.
It tricked.
It deceived. Even one who prayed and read the Bible,
faithfully, was not immune to that immovability. Vincent knew,
too well, that deciphering Spirit was a gift.
And how does one know when one has a gift—when it's

invisible?

Feeling? Sense? Reason?
All seeming antithesis to Spirit…yet…there were other kinds of
spirit. Vincent read Job so faithfully he could feel his fingertip
nerves burning—
yet even Job…had those whispering visitors…
          It seemed to Vincent it was in lamentation that one was
weakest and most vulnerable to the wrong kinds of spirit. And
he knew, from a physical view, he was not very strong.
          Yet, he painted
—fighting the wind through the canvas that hit back against his
every brushstroke—for God
didn't ever say it would be easy.
In fact He said it would cost one their very life
          —and everything they loved. Could he be blessed that
much?

He painted the rise,
etched the fall;
drove in the light where he'd painted too much darkness.
          His stomach pained him.
          He did not pray before taking a drink of wine
                    —he didn't have time—the wind was drying the
          paint
          and the paint wasn't right.
He knew when it was right.

He knew when he was finished and the light was beginning to fade...
he'd spent the entire day—there was just a little more to go... surely God would show him the way...
There
—there it came—bursting forth from the fibers of elemental space!
As brilliant before his eyes as he dreamt the creation of time itself was for God.
"Thank you!" he screamed to the heavens.
Heavens swelling with rain
—rain that swelled into pregnant water—that rounded and gathered
(skin)
until they fell...to the earth.

He did not think Sien would be there. But she was there, waiting. She took his wet coat. When her finger's skin grazed his throat he winced. His nerves were so sensitive it hurt.
Sien thought that the touch of her disgusted him—it disgusted her too...how low she'd become. So she said nothing—but made every effort to keep her touch from touching him again. Which, obviously, put her in a rather practical imposition, as she was there to seduce him.
Vincent collapsed in the chair. The only chair. There was but a dusting of coal left and Sien could see the man was soaked through his clothes.
She'd noticed
(earlier, when she'd shaken the place down—from rafter to floorboard—for money...or food)
there was a pipe and alongside it a pouch of tobacco.
"Would you like your pipe," she asked.
His eyes had already closed. He half-opened them with surprise. As if he'd forgotten her presence beside him, but nodded.
Sien loaded it (as she'd seen her father do—many times) but when she tried to hand it to him his arms were limp— his eyes had closed, again. She sighed. Staring at the thin, thin man before her. "If he dies," she thought, "then Theo

would still inherit..." but before she allowed herself that fruition, she lit the pipe in her own mouth without a single hesitation as if something beyond

     moved her mouth

         —to puff   puff   puff   the flame

         into the dried leaves—to puff puff puff

until the cheap, harsh ashsmoke filtered through the closed man's eyes

     (those eyes which lived, wide awake, behind the
     physical world of dying)

...and he stirred...so very slightly that Sien feared it was too late.

     And she didn't know why she cared.

     Her fate rested on his—his demise meant her liberation—in fact, she could...smother him...she knew she could...starved as he was—as starved as she was herself, she knew she had more strength than he...

     and yet those eyes...

     the kindness of them...

     the gentleness of his voice...

she found herself as able to harm him as a baby—sheep. "There," she saw her body rise, lifting the pipe to his lips, "this will help."

     He breathed. And smoke ringed his fire-damp hair.

***

The Priest, Father Thomas van Luijtelaar, was—as priests go—rather a humanist. So when he heard of the new Pastor's coming

> (and every detail of the new Pastor's life—including the fact that he had an older wife, a businessman son, unmarried daughters who'd come of age—and a deranged [estranged and lunatic] son)

he decided that the situation called—from a Christian point of view—for brotherly charity, instead of denominational politics. However, when Father Thomas

> (having taken the first opportunity to visit Pastor Theodorus—who'd found this move to be more physically exerting than any he'd done before…thus, even after having several weeks time, was surrounded by unpacked things atop every floor)

knocked on the pastor's door, Father Thomas found the pastor was not only terse

> (as Theodorus was—while greeting his nemesis— kicking some books behind the door with his feet)

…but rude: the Pastor hadn't even invited him in…for tea. And this did not go over well.
***

Two days Vincent went in and out of sleep while Sien
kept watch.
Two days.
She'd given him the last drop of wine.
What could she do?
If she stayed, they'd both die.

So she went into the street—she took the beatings from
the streetwalkers who cursed her for being younger and more
pretty than they were...but who ultimately quit hitting her for it
cost them too much energy—and it did not take very long

(an hour or two or three...Sien soon realized that the
men of the Hague liked who they liked and once a
customer always a customer)

before a young man, being drug along by his father by the nape
of his collar, came up to her. "How much?"
"Uh...uh" Sien didn't know what to say.
"Okay, then here!"

He handed his son some money and, swervingly, walked
away. The boy could not look Sien in the eye. For this, she
was thankful. But shyness only holds young men so long and
even though he did not look at her, straight on, he stared at her
dress—her breasts—and muttered something.
"Well," Sien thought, "this is it. I've become."

She took the boy's hand, leading him behind a building
and let him do whatever he wanted. Which wasn't much and
didn't take long before his eyes grew wide.

Just before he ran away he threw his money at her,
where it landed on the ground. Sien bent down...then quickly
gathered it up and went straight to
the baker's...
and the wine merchant's...
and the butcher's:

in her arms she carried all she'd gotten for her own
pound of flesh.
***

Pastor Theodorus heard, via the grapevine—or Creeping Charlie...or nettling gorse—that Father Thomas had, during Mass, vehemently condemned those who acted without brotherly charity. He knew exactly what the pontifical priest was up to...he was trying to poison the well.

"Well," Pastor Theodorus thought, "If this is how he wants it—so be it!"

After all, there was only one week until Easter Sunday—the biggest affair for the church (except, perhaps, Christmas) and Pastor Theodorus decided, then and there, that *his* Easter Sunday sermon would be one for the books.

"In fact," he thought, "If I know myself—and what I can do—I might even publish a tract after this. Now...what to preach? Easter...the Risen Lord...hope for tomorrow...but damn! I don't know this town or these people...but people are all the same...the uniting refrain:...SIN!"

***

The smell of cooking meat rousted Vincent, but not in
the way Sien had hoped. He rose, stumbled to the
washbasin—and vomited, then collapsed to the floor.
"Dear God!" she thought, "He is going to die."

She took the meat from the fire
(she'd paid too dear a price for it to let it burn)

then lifted Vincent's head, rubbing some wine on his lips,
brushing the hair from his stickycold forehead and whispered,
"Please don't die, Vincent. Please don't die."

Somewhere…
in the cavernous labyrinth he found himself lost within inside his
own frail humanity…he heard a sweetness

…a melody…

a beckoning

—like Ulysses' Sirens he feared—

(yet, as Homer understood

[as did he]

there were stronger things than hubris)

—and the sound of her…echoed him into consciousness.
***

In spite of the fact that four pews (total) were all that filled to hear Pastor Theodorus' words, he felt the Easter Sunday service went well. He'd felt particularly pleased with his rhetoric, his delivery, and his special attention to the Eucharist.

Father Thomas (while not able to boast such a meager crowd) felt equally proud.

And God, knowing all, watched men preaching from His pulpits.

***

"How long was I asleep?" Vincent asked.
"A long time."

Sien handed him a plate of meat. Again, Vincent vomited. Sien took a spoonful of meat broth, heated a bowl of water, and added it in.
"You must eat this."

He tried to refuse. But Sien would not hear of it. It took many spoonfuls and many bowls

> (which all, at first, ended up in the basin—and thrown into the cobbled street, to soak into the earth below them…feeding the beetles, cockroaches and worms)

before the brown liquid could be held down.

Then the diarrhea came. It was violent and painful—but the man never screamed—he simply bore on…and on…until Sien was sure God would kill him…if not out of mercy, then pity.   And then…even that was gone.

And then…his eyes looked a little less sunken. But, already…their supplies had run out. Sien knew that if she didn't get more food—all would have been in vain: so out to the street…and return again…only this time, when she returned, he was awake.
"Will he beat me for what I've done?" she wondered, "God I wish he would—I deserve to die…but if I hadn't have, then…"
"It's okay," Vincent said, rising from his chair. "You've nothing to fear from me. But I'd like to talk to you, if you don't mind?"

She set the bread and wine and meat on the table then sat at his feet.

He read to her from the Bible in order that she might learn of Jesus' grace
—believing she'd not heard it before—

> (though she had: all her life…in church…beside the parents who preferred her dead). At his feet she listened to him read:

> "Romans I, 14-17:
> I am debtor both to the Greeks, and to the Barbarians; both to the wise, and to the unwise. So as much as in me is, I am ready to preach the gospel to you that are at Rome also. For I am not ashamed of the gospel of Christ:

for it is the power of God unto salvation to every one that believeth; to the Jew first, and also to the Greek. For therein is the righteousness of God revealed from faith to faith: as it is written, The just shall live by faith."

Vincent lifted her chin, meeting her eyes to his. "I understand what you did—maybe even why you did it. But you must not...anymore. Do you understand?"
"But you would have died!"
Sien began sobbing. She'd had no one to tell that her stomach, her womb, had been hurting and that she was filled with fear about what was soon to come.
"Then I would have died." Vincent replied, without a single blinked eye. "There are worse things than death."
"Not for me."
"That's because you don't comprehend what you're saying. You see," he softened, climbing onto the floor to sit beside her, "I can not die. I am eternal...because Christ already died for me."
She shook her head back and forth, slowly, but adamantly: "That makes absolutely...no sense."
He grinned. "Listen:

I Corinthians, 11:
'Be ye followers of me, even as I also am of Christ. Now I praise you, brethren, that ye remember me...'"

Sien felt herself drifting off to sleep. She rested her head against Vincent's shoulder as he still read:

'...in all things, and keep the ordinances, as I delivered them to you. But I would have you know, that the head of every man is Christ; and the head of the woman is the man; and the head of Christ is God."

She murmured, "That sounds nice."
He asked, "Would you like me to read on?"
"Yes...yes..."
'Every man praying or prophesying, having his head covered, dishonoreth his head. But every woman that prayeth or

prophesieth with her head uncovered dishonoreth her head: for that is even all one as if she were shaven. For if the woman be not covered, let her also be shorn: but if it be a shame for a woman to be shorn or shaven, let her be covered. For a man indeed ought not to cover his head, forasmuch as he is the image and glory of God: but the woman is the glory of the man. For the man is not of the woman; but the woman for the man. For this cause ought the woman to have power on her head because of the angels. Nevertheless neither is the man without the woman, neither the woman without the man, in the Lord. For as the woman is of the man, even so is the man also by the woman; but all things of God. Judge in yourselves: is it comely that a woman pray unto God uncovered? Doth not even nature itself teach you, that, if a man have long hair, it is a shame unto him? But if a woman have long hair, it is a glory to her: for her hair is given her for a covering. But if any man seem to be contentious, we have no such custom, neither the churches of God. Now in this that I declare unto you I praise you not, that ye come together not for the better, but for the worse. For first of all, when ye come together in the church, I hear that there be divisions among you; and I partly believe it. For there must be also heresies among you, that they which are approved may be made manifest among you. When ye come together therefore into one place, this is not to eat the Lord's supper. For in eating every one taketh before other his own supper: and one is hungry, and another is drunken. What? Have ye not houses to eat and to drink in? or despise ye the church of God, and shame them that have not? What shall I say to you? Shall I praise you in this? I praise you not.'

Vincent looked at Sien's rising chest. The life inside her—beneath her dress—he could only imagine...as starving as her own face betrayed...the poor infant...and it pained him worse than any physical pain...so he prayed,
"God, what am I to do? I can't let her starve. I can't let her do what she does...and yet I, myself, have no money. I can't care for her. What am I to do...Dear God...what do You want me to do!"

His eyes, as if by nature, returned to the page:

'For I have received of the Lord that which also I delivered
unto you, That the Lord Jesus the same night in which he was
betrayed took bread: and when he had given thanks, he brake
it, and said, Take, eat: this is my body, which is broken for
you: do this in remembrance of me.'

"Dear God," Vincent cried out, waking Sien, "I am broken for
You too. Help me! Please."

Sien looked at Vincent's face. It was contorted in a pain
like none she'd seen before—like anguish…but then—when he
noticed she'd wakened—it passed.
"More?" he asked—lifting the Bible up.
"Sure," she said—all sleep driven out by the zealousness of
what had just happened—and the fear that if she said she'd
heard enough something…dreadful…would happen.

'After the same manner also he took the cup, when he had
supped, saying, This cup is the new testament in my blood:
this do ye, as oft as ye drink it, in remembrance of me. For as
often as ye eat this bread, and drink this cup, ye do shew the
Lord's death till he come. Wherefore whosoever shall eat this
bread, and drink this cup of the Lord, unworthily, shall be
guilty of the body and blood of the Lord. But let a man
examine himself, and so let him eat of that bread, and drink of
that cup. For he that eateth and drinketh unworthily, eateth
and drinketh damnation to himself, not discerning the Lord's
body. For this cause many are weak and sickly among you,
and may sleep. For if we would judge ourselves, we should
not be judged. But when we are judged, we are chastened of
the Lord, that we should not be condemned with the world.
Wherefore, my brethren, when ye come together to eat, tarry
one for another. And if any man hunger, let him eat at home:
that ye come not together unto condemnation. And the rest
will I set in order when I come.'

Then Vincent ate. And drank. And was filled with a
happiness Sien hadn't seen in him (though she hadn't been

around him very much) for he was filled—satiated—content…in body and spirit.

And when he was savoring the very last morsel of meat on his plate he exclaimed,
"I know what's to be done!"

and, grabbing his coat, he nearly ran from the house.
***

Meanwhile, in Paris, Theo was having a bit of trouble. It seemed that the art business was going through one of its 'downturns' and, as always with such events, the owners began to get more 'observant' of every cent spent. This was not good. For Theo, having had unchecked access to company funds, had spent a great deal

—borrowing some (though without lending notes)— knowing that 'soon' the turn would turn right and the market would brighten.

Meanwhile, up top, the art of the artists whom Theo swore were 'tops' began stacking up…against the walls.

However, Goupil was not in the position (yet) to require such scrutiny of every asset—so, for the time being, Theo's 'stashing' was safe. Though he longed for the relief his pending marriage would bring…only…he hadn't yet informed his parents.

Why?

Well, such things can't be rushed. He'd already suffered the rake of his father with regard to his choice in career.

He could see it all now, "Manufacturers!"

> (his mind even conjured the image of his father waving his arms like a fish, flailing, caught, and could hear the further lectures on the cost of wealth).

He didn't feel up to bearing it.

Besides, there was still See…and Vincent…and if things went as planned the timing would be grand: for when Vincent announced such a misfortunate union how could his parents, then, object to his marriage—in fact, he bemused, they'd be pleased!
***

At Anton's house, Vincent was met by Jet.

"Good afternoon, Cousin," she said, "What brings you here?"

He twisted his hat. He'd never done this before. "Good Cousin, may I come in?"

She looked over her shoulder. There was something uneasy about her. "No, Vincent," she said. "Wait."

She closed the door, but quickly returned with her shawl. "I'll be back shortly," she called, then took her cousin's arm. "Let's walk," she said.

And they did.

Vincent told her of all that had happened to him and how he'd met Sien. And how miraculous God was—to bring them together—and that, by making her an honest woman...by saving her from the streets...he'd be doing just what God would want any man to do.

Jet, having no knowledge of Anton's confession, grew quite pale. "You mean the girl I met that night?"

"Yes, Jet. Yes. Sien. And she's going to have a baby."

Jet's grasp loosened from Vincent's arm. He ushered her to the nearest bench. "Cousin? Are you okay?"

"Vincent, do you know what you're saying?"

"I do. I do, Jet. I really do. I prayed and read the Bible. And I know in my heart it's the right thing to do."

She knew, in such a fervor, there was no dissuading him. "So why did you come to visit me?"

"Well," he said, returning to twisting his cap, "I need...some...money."

She immediately gave him what little she had upon her person and after he'd walked her back to her home she, without hesitation, wrote to her cousin, Theo,

> (to whom she'd been told was responsible for Vincent's care)

that he'd become quite thin and, in her opinion, dangerously mentally ill.

***

Upon receipt of Jet's letter Theo drafted one of his own. Though naked and filled with absinthe (and a woman's tongue frequently down his throat) he wrote:

Dear Father,

> *I'm sorry to inform you that Vincent is unwell—in mind—according to our cousin (with whom you entrusted his care). So I will travel to the Hague as soon as possible to assess the situation and report to you what I find there.*

> *Your Loving Son,*
> *Theo.*

Quickly sealed—it would have to wait for the next day's post—for tongues can only go so long…without kneading.
***

"Sien," Vincent was as if a child on a day he'd gotten what he'd really wanted, "I have money. You don't have to do what you do anymore…and I want you to marry me."

This…was not what Sien was expecting.

If anything could be more startling for her, she did not know what.

In fact, she half thought

(after his lengthy reading of the Bible) that he had walked out…never to return. But then he was home,

and more,

asking her to marry him.

"But…I'm with child. Another man's."

"I know and I don't care!"

"You don't care? How can you not care? It will ruin your family, your father…"

She stopped herself cold—he'd not told her that his father was a pastor.

"I don't care. It's the right thing to do."

"But," she felt almost too scared to ask, "do you…love me?"

"Love you! Of course! You are my fellow wretched Sister. You, who've suffered the worst injustice—who should have already been married to the man,"

he pointed to her stomach,

"and believe me, Sien, he will pay for such sin. But I know enough to know God doesn't make mistakes and he brought us together for a reason. Oh Sien!"

He fell to his knees, throwing his arms around her waist. He rested his head against her swollen belly. "Don't you see? I'll be the father. No one will know. You and I will be…"

She blushed.

"Oh…I didn't mean…that. I meant…well…"

She lifted his chin so that his eyes met hers. "Why not that?"

It was the first time she actually wanted to.

"No," he said, firmly.

But women have their ways.

The—
      let the line slacken...
                     let them feel they aren't fighting...
          then quietly reel them in...
as they glide,
      slowly swashing
their tales
      in water that feels
—ever so slightly—turgid

      ...until
            they're
hooked...good
***

Jo Bonger was,
again,
visiting Paris (and her intended). She was shopping,
again,
for her wedding clothes
(and spending an obscene amount of money. Though
her father objected, her mother demanded: both
recognized their daughter's genealogical emeritus).
Besides, she'd quickly learned
(having quickly discerned Theo's lifestyle and tastes)
that the surest way for her to be foremost in his thoughts was to
frequent his place of business—and purchase…expensively
overpriced 'neu veaux' art
(of which Theo had amassed a rather large collection of)
plus she liked the "pretty colors."
Theo, more than happy was ecstatic, to see his
betrothed at the door. For he'd just
—only moments before—
posted his letter to his father about Vincent.
"Oh Jo! I can't wait," he said, indiscreetly embracing her and
kissing her lips.
"Theo!" She pushed him away.
He'd forgotten etiquette. But that mattered little as they,
almost playfully, climbed the stairs to 'the' store (though once
on the second floor Theo—once or twice—had to make
footroom…for the canvases littered nearly every square foot
of…the quickly cramping space).
"You know," he said, "this one is quite fine." And held up one
by Paul Gauguin.
"Yes. Yes," she replied, "I see what you mean. I'll take that
one…oh and what about that over there?"
She pointed to a landscape thick with impasto.
"That?"
He pointed to make sure he'd heard right.
"Yes. That! With the colors. Oh…isn't that red…and that
green…it's almost like brightness…"
"Oh Jo, you don't know what you're talking about. Try this
one," he said, holding up a Monet.
"Oh I don't know. I really sort of…"
"Try the Monet."

His tone seemed insistent (though she thought the price exorbitant—especially because the colors weren't nearly so…vibrant).

She couldn't have known that his very contract (with Monet that is) depended upon the sale. Besides, what did it matter to her other than pleasing him? So she bought the Monet and the Gauguin and some other Dutch and French artists (whom she'd never heard of) and set about,

once again,

to her shopping for linen and fabric and hats and shoes and…

***

When Sien's fingers touched the skin beneath his chin it was as if some vague memory told his nerves—all firing—that he'd known such a thing before. As if some voltage were warning him. Though he tried to resist, tried to focus on the fact that he would be doing what was right in God's eyes...her skin touching his...was electrifying.

And then she (upon meeting his resistance to stand) fell to her knees in front of him so...that there on the floor (both being dwarfhigh—as if their legs had never grown) there was nothing of height between them.

Nothing but breath.

And Vincent thought (but did not speak it), "Dear God...help me...resist." But he knew himself better than this...so that when she put her arms around his neck and gently kissed his lips he cried, "I'm falling, Lord, I'm falling...and I don't want to be saved..."

And when she laid back upon the wood (spreading her legs) he cried tears upon her long black hair for he knew her...knew her...then...there...and felt the black of her hair as if webs of inked sin...weeping and dying his soul.
***

Pastor Theodorus received Theo's letter with such a shock that he felt his heart would burst in his chest and immediately made haste to travel to The Hague.

When he arrived, he was horrified at what he found: his son, prostrate on the ground
(covered in blood from his own chastisement—the knotted leather whip still clenched in his hand)
and a woman of ill-repute hastening to dress herself in his presence.

"What in God's name is going on here?"

Vincent tried to stand but weaved, as if drunk, and fell.

Sien, torn between rushing to him and dressing herself, opted to cover what she could in the presence of an obviously pious man.

Vincent murmured, "Father...I love her..."

The man's eyes. If there could be an animus captured—those eyes would have been a bull enraged, a cat's claw, a scent-release from any foul creature—there was such hatred in them for her.

She cowered. Slowing, sliding her clothes to her cover.

"I...am..." he spat the words at her, "Vincent's father, Pastor Theodorus van Gogh, and I am taking him away from this place—and YOU—FOREVER!"

He clenched his fist at her, shaking as if possessed by the devil himself.

She'd never been so afraid in all her life—so she ran to the street (for even the streetwalker's fury seemed kinder).

Alone, Theodorus held his son. "Vincent, my boy, what have you done to yourself?"

He tried to raise him. But Vincent lay prone, murmuring, "Father...forgive me," he began to cry, "I've...sinned."

The pastor spat again, "Those kind of women! Those kind of women! I've seen them ruin the best kind of men."

Then he softened, seeing the blood of his son, "It's only natural to sin, Vincent. It's sin that you're feeling—the worst kind I fear. But I'm taking you home now. It will all be better there...we can take care of you..."

"No Father," Vincent tried to raise himself—but he felt so woozy, so unsteady, as if his very blood coursed some vile fermented fruit.

149

In the coach, Theodorus worried over his son. It was as if Vincent had been poisoned. Vincent fell, quickly, into disturbed and tormented dreams. His father held his body against him, whispering comfort and praying—praying to cast out the demons, which had taken hold of the man his boy had become.

When he'd finally brought Vincent home
> (having required assistance when they'd changed
> transports...for Vincent never once, during the
> trip, became fully lucent)

he and Cor carried him up to bed.

Pastor Theodorus wasn't even sure his son knew where he was or if he would notice that he was in a place he'd never been before—for, in fact, the family was still settling into...his newly assigned parish.

His mother was beside herself. She'd never seen anyone as ill as her Vincent was. The doctor was immediately sent for. But having heard Theodorus' account of his 'living' arrangements was convinced. He was treated for "such" things as not proper to name in the presence of women and put on a strict, bland diet.

His mother made a thin potato soup. For not only did she know how much he enjoyed eating potatoes (filled with hot steam) as a child, but Theo had brought one of his paintings home to her...a family sitting down to a plate of potatoes. She looked up at the painting she'd hung on the bedroom wall—seeing those eyes, those Dutch eyes, and those...potatoes...and thinking, "That's my Vincent. Only him."

But he took only a little soup. It wasn't his body's illness...it was his mother's touch. "Don't," he said, weakly pulling her hand from the back of his head—where she'd been propping him up.
"Why, Vincent? Why won't you let me help you?"

He could see tears in her eyes. He didn't want to hurt her...more...than he'd already done...but he could never tell her the truth.
"Because...I...am...unwell."
"I know Son. That's why I want to help you."

He gathered his every strength to sit. His one leg muscle spasmed—his other cramped. "Leave me!" he shouted.

She fled. It was the first time he saw fear in his mother's eyes. But he did not ponder them long…for almost immediately thereafter…he slept.

Three days.

Each hour his mother came to him, to his delusional dream-but-waking face and forced sips of water to his lips.

Three days…

she cleaned his cheeks, his forehead, his neck but Pastor Theodorus was insistent that he tend to the rest of the man. For he had not told her of her son's own chastisement…nor of his fear that his son's self-inflicted lashing wounds were, in fact, becoming infected.

The doctor was recalled. He freshly dressed Vincent's wounds. His serious glances at the father were enough to convey. There was much to be concerned of—the doctor was insistent that Theodorus stay with his son at all times, until the fever broke, and he was to change the dressings every hour— reapplying the special salve (he'd only just patented) which was claimed to repel gangrene.

The father prayed, incessantly. An act he'd not found himself prone to performing…since his first Vincent had died.

He prayed, "Am I worse than King David?"

He cried, not knowing his wife was listening at the door.

She was a kind soul—and never liked suffering. "Let me watch now," she said. Noticing that her husband, though younger than she, looked much more aged.
"No. I must not. The doctor insisted."
"But you're exhausted, dear. Besides. There's someone here to see you."

And there was:

  a field worker's wife was at the door—her husband was

    dead [cut during harvest,
    the wound {not mortally deep}
    had infected|infection spread]
    and, being one of the few Protestants,
    required the pastor's burial service.

He was obliged. For no matter what the needs of ones fleshly family—a Pastor's first duty was to his church.

And Vincent's mother was glad for the chance. Almost as soon as her husband had left the room she lifted Vincent's shirt, gasping!

Vincent's eyes opened. "Go away." He did not have the strength to command it.

"No Son. I will not. You tell me why you've done this."

He could not resist, for he'd wanted…all that time…to confess…and illness had taken from him his inhibitions.

"I am a man. There is a woman. Her name is Sien and I love her. I want to marry her and be the father of her child."

Anna van Gogh's eyes teared with joy! Her eldest boy had found a wife. She'd secretly wondered (after some previous romantic faux paus) if he'd ever be blessed with domestic life. "Oh joy, Vincent. Joy!"

"Mother…she's a…prostitute."

Her eyes kept right on crying.

But Vincent's closed. He could not bear to witness his penance.

***

Though the van Gogh doctor was sure it was his special salve (asking Theodorus to endorse it) that had saved Vincent's life, Vincent's mother knew that Vincent's recovery had been nothing short of a miracle.

Secretly, Anna van Gogh was hoping that her son's "little confession" was simply the effect of his near-death illness. This hope was, quickly thereafter, shattered. For as soon as he was able to walk, Vincent called his family together

(his sisters Anna, Wil and Lies as well as his little brother Cor)

and announced he was going to marry Sien.

Theodorus, like his wife, had hoped that recovery had driven such madness from his mind. That such a miracle

(the miracle God had revealed to Pastor Theodorus ~via the field worker's tragedy~ in order for him to see just

how dangerous Vincent's infected-condition had been)

surely meant that God had driven the demons from his son's tormented spirit.

But there he stood, in front of all of them, weak and skinny but alive—declaring his love for a woman of ill-repute. Vincent knew their sensibilities. He knew them all too well— inside himself.

"I know you think I'm mad but please listen to me. She and I are more than what we have become." He thrust his hands up and down the outside of his body, sides, front, back. "If you judged me by what I am before you, you would say I am fouled, I am a remnant of a man. But you KNOW this is not true. You know this because you love me."

Anna van Gogh began crying.

Still, Vincent continued, "And just as you know that of me...I know that of her."

"But Vincent," Theodorus' voice began to give way with emotion, "we just can't...this is too much..."

"How many times do we forgive father? How many times? And did not Jesus himself save a prostitute?"

"But DAMN IT!" Theodorus, for the first time in all his life, cursed in front of his children and wife, "You're not JESUS!"

"Father we're all Jesus."

"I'll not have this blasphemy in my house!"

Knowing his son too weak to leave, he removed himself.

153

Storming to his parish. Brewing.

How he hated the indignant righteousness—the piousness—of his son.

"How dare he," he swore, pounding his fist into the palm of his free hand, "Who does he think he is? He is mad to think we'd ever consent to such a union…it would ruin…oh my God! My parish! We'd be cast out for sure…then what? How would we survive? A pastor's son marrying a prostitute…nonono…it can NEVER happen! He's mad. This time he asks too much!"

Theodorus drafted a:

"Dear Theo…"

but before he could send it…he died.

At the funeral Elder Vincent
  (to whom Theo had been making constant
 application to)
held condemning eyes upon his godson,
his namesake,
his nephew
  —the whoremonger whose scandal would be the
 unraveling of all that his beloved brother
  (the upstanding pastor) had stood for—.
Vincent thought it ironic that, in his death, his father had suddenly become more to his surviving elder brother
  (for unbeknownst to Theo or Uncle Cent, there had been
 times when Pastor Theodorus had confessed: [to
 Vincent—when he was in his evangelism] of sensing,
 always, a great deal of rivalry…more from his older
 brother to him than the other way round)
than he had been in life.
 Of course there were his father's other brothers to be faced: Stricker and Cor—and the chorus complete with his own sister, Anna, in tow:
  all condemning Vincent's despicable notion of marrying
  a whore as the impetus for the death, the sore loss of
(as Elder Vincent read from his notes)
"A most reputable man who did his best to keep order and to keep his fold safe from the wolves of the world."
 Vincent, audibly laughed.

This would have proven Vincent's undoing
(for Theo had already told Elder Vincent that his father's
very last request was that Vincent be institutionalized)
had it not been for the strength Vincent's mother found growing
within herself from the moment her husband died. And she
would not hear of it.

However, it was obvious that Vincent could not be
trusted to be alone. So she and Theo
(Theo being then the eldest male—in reasonable mind)
sat down to discuss the future plans for Vincent's care.   Theo
said one word, "Arles."

He told his mother that he'd learned, from his 'artists,'
about certain places. Places where people do more to help
than others.

He did not tell his mother that there were places, certain
places, where people are less to each other—and that such a
place was where he knew his brother would
founder...particularly (savoring the fall of a saint) as he'd
already acquired a taste for flesh.
***

In Arles there were women.

In Arles there was Absinthe.

In Arles there was an outlawish sense to the scene.

In Arles there were houses.

In Arles there were cafes.

In Arles there were plenty of scenes…

and the heat of the Midi…

the strength of the wind…

in Arles there was plenty of everything/nothing…

in Arles there was loneliness…

in Arles there was promise…

in Arles there were PAINTINGS!

And then…there was the 3rd betrayal: that of Friend.

The decision was made: St. Remy.

"Brother, I ask but one thing of you," Vincent pled.
"What, Vincent?"
"Let me be with Sien when she births the child."
     Theo shook his head thinking:
"Of all the things to beg for—when everything has been stripped (including his—substantial—inheritance) all he can think of is her."
     For a moment he thought he felt a surge…was it…jealousy? After all, she had been…so long ago…his Dutch Beauty…but that was—then.
"Fine. But only if you agree to commit yourself without one more, single, problem."
"Fine."
"Oh," Theo added, "I'll be sending you paint supplies. How many canvases do you think you can finish before you leave to see…her?"
"I'm not sure. I've not been well. You know this. But I'll work as hard as I can."
"I know, Brother." Theo smiled. "I know."
     but he must work himself harder…to death
***

The hospital was small, out of the way, still expensive.

He had not seen Sien since he'd left the Hague with his father. The nurse insisted that the woman before him was Sien. At first, Vincent did not believe her: she was unrecognizable.

If before she was thin—she'd become less.

If before her eyes wore dark circles—they'd sunk to such depths he knew not human orifices could.

He started to cry, but she shushed him.
The baby was sleeping at her side.

He went to her, kissing her forehead, noticing

—the gloss of her black hair had dulled. There were bald patches.
She smiled and said "Thank you" revealing that one of her front teeth had fallen...
"I didn't think I'd ever see you again," she said.
"Neither did I, you."

He could not look her in the eye.
"You promised you'd marry me, remember?"
"I do. I want to...I still want to..."

See knew. She knew it was stronger than they were.
"It's okay, Vincent. You can't save me."
"But Sien..."

She shushed him again—then held the baby out to him. His hands trembled. The baby's boyeyes opened: two little whitish blue things...like puppyeyes...and the infant's fingers grasped at what he could not see

—clasping upon the roughened, stained finger of the man who held him—

{the sobbing man} whose tears fell,

one

by

one,

to barely soak the swaddling cloth wrapped round: that which had been donated to the hospital for bastard children of indigent women.

***

St. Remy had been chosen, by Theo, strategically.

If there was one thing one's closest relations know—it's how to strike close. For St. Remy was run by Catholics. Oh there were doctors and nurses (and attendants…to be sure) but it was the Nuns, the Sisters, the Papacy itself that determined life in St. Remy.

Theo had learned, from his life as a Protestant's son, that there was one sure way to drive a Protestant zealot crazy—leave them to the Catholics|Nuns.

He had not planned on Tommy.

***

"I am here to see Messr van Gogh."

"Your name?"

"Messr Thomas McGill."

"Occupation?"

"Minister."

"Really?" Dr. Peyron looked the rather-young man up from head to toe.

"Yes," the young man replied.

"Where are you from?"

"The Borinage Coal Fields, Belgium."

"What brings you all the way here?"

"Messr van Gogh."

"I see. And what is your interest with him?"

"I've known him all of my life."

"Funny," Dr. Peyron replied, "He's never mentioned you."

"Well," said the young man, "It's been a very long time."

He was led to Vincent's [cell|room]. What the young man found mortified him. Not so much because he'd not grown thick sensibilities when it came to human suffering—he'd been an evangelist enough years by then—it was simply that the man before him...having once been a giant (a man greatly enlarged by his fight for the humanity of miners)...had grown...so...small. As if he cowered...

"Vincent," Thomas went to him, "You probably don't remember me."

The man shook his head.

Thomas thought he seemed almost...childlike.

"They're coming! I can hear them!" Vincent screamed.

"Who? Who is coming?"

"The demons! Those hellbound wenches to torment me—they give me no peace!"

Thomas knew a lost soul when he saw one. It was his memories...his recollections of what had been that made him blind at first..."I know you've accepted Christ..."

"He's abandoned me! There is no God! I'm all alone in this place left to die!"

Thomas grabbed Vincent's head

—his hands on both sides—

"Hear me Brother! There are fates worse than dying!"

And he held out a drawing…
                an artifact from long   long   ago—

                like a beaconing
                        light atop a deep dark water…
it flittered down…
                                down…
                                        Down.

It was Evangelist.

"Tommy?" Vincent
                finally
                        looked up—
                        could finally see
beyond the persecution of the religion he'd been bound within

"Is…is that you?"
"Yes, Vincent. Yes. I came as soon as I heard what had
happened to you."
                Suddenly aware of himself—like Adam to God after
Falling—he pressed his hands up and down his chest. "I look
terrible…I've suffered…"
"You look no worse than I did when you delivered me."
"Delivered you?"
"Yes. That's what I came to tell you. I prayed the whole way
that I would not be too late."
"I don't understand. Are you taking me out of here?"
"Perhaps."
"I…"
"Yes…you. It's because of you that I became an evangelist."

"You're…Evangelist?"

        The young man could see how thinly the shreds of veiled
reality were to which the broken man clung.
"Yes, Vincent…and so are you."

"Me?" he beamed.   "ME! Evangelist?   But he's
so…   so beautiful…   and blessed…and
guided by God instead of…"
"It's called The Slough of Despond—remember?"

    Vincent smiled.

It had been a long   long   time.   So   long
    ago

      that the words
           had faded…to where…
        to where had his mind gone?
So long and yet, instantly returned…
"Can God ever forgive…me? I knew…yet chose…to leave."
"Are you confessing your sins to me, Vincent?"
"I suppose. Isn't that what I do?"

    The young man's eyes bleared. Could a man be
brought so low as this? "Not to me. To God."
"But they said I couldn't."
"Who said you couldn't?"
"They…"
    he pointed a shaky finger towards the locked door.

The young man opened his Bible—

reading passage after passage

    where God's word drenched
a land gone cracked and brittle with drought—
and it filled that which had been broken,
flooding it over

so that the barren scorched dust of the man
(being so long without…that he'd forgotten how to thirst)
began, again…   to   drink   the Living Water.
***

He was painting:
     the crows circling—
     ᴧ as they always did ᴧ
     then landing,
     pecking,
     using their wings on the varying strengths of the wind

when there came upon him something powerful.
     Something he'd never experienced before
         and every nerve in his body focused into one
     burning
         pressure within him.

He looked to the sun:
     —and though it burnt with summer hot—
it appeared to dim.

In the distance he thought he saw his brother.

He wanted to call to him but felt unable to do anything but
                             succumb.

When he rose. The late-light of summersky was graying.

He did not want to leave his easel, his paints:
     he'd paid so much for them.
But something pressed him to move,
     like an infant being compelled to take its first breath,
and that was when he felt the stickiness of his own blood.

     It was Christian's journey all over again:
the Slough of Despair,
the Worldly Wiseman
and he remembered,
"If it is the hard—but right way, I will hope to endure..."

yet his thoughts could not coalesce upon a singularity.
His feet felt lead.
He fell to the ground.

He thought he saw Evangelist waving to him, in the distance,
giving him strength to carry on.

So he crawled.

And then there was the Shining Gate,
but when he put his hand to the wood
there was blood on his hand.

Yet the door opened, easily, and he saw people.
He was ashamed,
for he knew that blood was seen to be dirty.
In the Borinage he'd learned:
one's appearance made the difference to people
struggling to survive.

So when Messr Ravoux asked if he was alright,

simply   his
Vincent   nodded   head

—an obedient servant—
and tried (with all the strength he still had)

effortless.
seem
stairs
the
up
assent
his
make
to

When he finally let his body fall, upon his singularly
narrow bed, he swore he heard Despair whisper,
"I could be anyone. I could even be you."

He noticed the other Dutch boarder disappear out of his room.

Before he fell into a deep sleep he rolled to his side
[with his back to the door] in order to keep whomever
might come, from the unpleasantness of his body's fluid.

Then the Shining One came in,
        holding a pen poised above a lined book,
"Put down your name," he commanded,
while at the same time withdrawing his sword.
Vincent cried out,
        "I think I know the meaning of this,"
        and to the paper, he signed, 'Vincent.'

Then a cross appeared in front of his eyes to which his body
—his very body—
replied in a singular release.
        As if every burden he carried upon his back
        and within his heart
        ceased to exist.
But…there was still something…gnawing at his…gut…

Time Passed.

Then, before his awakening eyes, sat his brother's calm
blue irises. Theo was placing a piece of paper into the pocket
of his coat. "You missed again," Vincent heard the words
escape his own throat.

"What do you mean, Brother?" Theo asked.
"I know."
　　　Theo rose and closed the door.

　　　Before his eyes, Vincent saw:
Timorous and Mistrust. "Don't be afraid,"
he said to the visions
　　　　　　(while Theo listened),
"But you're going the wrong way.
Ahead of you there are lions
and demons and all sorts of dangers."

Theo scoffed then replied, "I'll tell Mother you died bravely…but
foolishly."

Vincent heard Watchful cry,
"Is your strength so small?"

　　　Then he saw Theo, again, standing, resting his shoulder
against the wall.
　　　The room was stifling hot.
"Like hell," he imagined.
　　　So he beckoned, with his finger, for Theo to come to his
side. "Brother," Vincent whispered, "Come closer."
"I'm close." Theo replied.
"Closer."
"How much closer can I be?"
"Share my bed with me."

For fear of Vincent making a fuss and attracting attention, the
brother obeyed [though the bed was too small to afford them to
lie separated from each other].

Vincent patted his chest
　　　　{after rolling back onto his back}
inviting his brother's head to rest there.

　　　Theo saw dried blood,
　　　smelled blood
　　　—but with disgust verging vomiting—
　　　did as his brother requested.
He'd already gone so far
(how much more would he have to endure?).

"Did you ever read 'Pilgrim's Progress'?" Vincent asked.
"Yes," Theo lied.

"Then I tell you Brother: I am Discretion. Your secret is safe
with me."

　　　Theo jumped from his brother's embrace, indignant.
"What do you mean?"
"There is no time for this. Much of what you see—my insides—
have been slashed and hacked away. This is, after all, the stuff
of war."
　　　Theo began to cry.
　　　He fell to his knees—at his brother's side.
　　　"Vincent. What do you want of me?"
"To avert the darts of the wicked one."

"I don't understand."
"You do."

　　　Then, as if a veil had been lifted from his eyes, Theo
saw—for the first time—all that he had done. And he wept,
inexorably—with the strength of Mercy and Charity."

"Oh God!" Theo cried out, "What have I done!"

Vincent murmured, "Though I walk through the Valley of the Shadow of Death, I will fear no evil, for Thou are with me."

Theo crawled back into the bed,
crying his salt into his brother's chest,
"Please, Vincent, don't go. Don't. Forgive me."

Vincent patted his little brother's head, "I already have. Now, Theo, I ask you...What Will You Buy?"
    "Nothing! Nothing again."
"No, Brother. You must—you must buy something...but it can only be The Truth."
"Yes, Vincent, anything you say."
"For we are," he kissed Theo's head, "two pilgrims on the way to the Celestial City...even though the World will call us madmen, just as they did Christian, do not despair for the path ahead of us is straight and true."

Theo sat up,
as if speaking in a different tongue,
and, desperately, replied:

"But
if I go
where you have gone,
I will lose my freedom."

"Yes, Theo, freedom to follow
Vanity Fair,
Mr. Moneylove,
Mr. Lovegain and Mr. Coveting!"

Vincent coughed and grabbed his stomach.
"Does it hurt...much," Theo asked.
"No.   Not if it is worthwhile. But...can I have my pipe?"

Theo got his pipe,
filling it with his own very fine, expensive tobacco
and held it out for his brother.

When Vincent tasted the tobacco,

that difference
—the disparity between his own and his brother's—

he was sore afraid

for he knew,
once such tastes had been rooted,
they grew...
and proliferated
like milkthistle...or mustard seed...

"Theo," he said, "It is late.　　　　I must go."

He breathed out
—exhaling deeper than life itself—
and Theo thought he saw
a Shining One, or an orb...or Tome...so he kissed his brother's
forehead. And felt, he swore, something warm against his own.
***

THE CASE OF THE MURDER OF VINCENT van GOGH

All great murder mysteries have to begin with…well, a murder.

MURDER OR MANSLAUGHTER?

It would be impossible to answer this question as it applies, first, to the death of Vincent van Gogh, second, in the year, 1890—and, finally, in France. However, by today's legal definitions in the USA (specifically, Texas—the home state of our *great* president) it may be less of a creative stretch than you might imagine. First, some definitions:

(According to Damien Falgoust at the University of Texas School of Law's course outline [for "Criminal Law"], 1996):

SECTION C.   THE TEXAS PENAL CODE DEFINITIONS OF CULPABLE MENTAL
STATES

1.   DEFINITIONS:

c.   RECKLESSLY – WITH RESPECT TO CIRCUMSTANCES OF
CONDUCT OR RESULT OF CONDUCT, PERSON <u>CONSCIOUSLY
DISREGARDS</u> A 'SUBSTANTIAL AND UNJUSTIFIABLE RISK
THAT CIRCUMSTANCES EXIST OR WILL OCCUR.' THE RISK
MUST BE SUCH THAT THERE IS A <u>GROSS DEVIATION</u> FROM AN
ORDINARY PERSON'S STANDARD OF CARE FROM THE
ACTOR'S VIEWPOINT."

1.   THE BOMB HYPO – THE ACTOR HAS 'RECKLESS'
INTENT WITH REGARD TO PEOPLE AT A NEARBY TABLE THAT
THE ACTOR DIDN'T BELIEVE THE BOMB WOULD BE
POWERFUL ENOUGH TO REACH.

d.   NEGLIGENTLY – WITH RESPECT TO CIRCUMSTANCES OF
CONDUCT, PERSON SHOULD BE AWARE OF A SUBSTANTIAL
AND UNJUSTIFIABLE RISK THAT CIRCUMSTANCES EXIST OR
THE RESULT WILL OCCUR. RISK MUST BE SUCH THAT THERE
IS A GROSS DEVIATION FROM AN ORDINARY PERSON'S
STANDARD OF CARE FROM THE ACTOR'S VIEWPOINT.

1.   THE BOMB HYPO – THE ACTOR HAS
'NEGLIGENT' INTENT WITH REGARD TO
PEDESTRIANS THE ACTOR DIDN'T THINK THE
BOMB COULD REACH.

Using either of the above definitions, Theo van Gogh would have been legally culpable, at least in part, for Vincent van Gogh's death. Especially considering the following:

Theo van Gogh disregarded Vincent's primary physician's, Dr. Peyron's, professional opinion that Vincent was not ready to leave the asylum at St. Rémy (Arles, France). Additionally, Vincent expressed serious concerns for his own welfare when the issue of being released from St. Remy was broached.

However, both men would change their positions. Vincent would vie for being released and Dr. Peyron would write, "Cured" in his notes for Vincent's records (which may, in fact, have been to relieve himself of culpability).

Both Dr. Peyron and Vincent were assured that Vincent would receive close supervision by both his brother and a physician specializing in melacholia, Dr. Gachet. Dr. Gachet took special interest in melancholia and had published articles about it.

Close supervision did not occur. Theo arranged for Vincent to live in Auvers-sur-Oise, which is, approximately, 22 miles from Paris. This means that in the late 1800s it would have taken a person somewhere between 2.17 and 2.71 hours to travel by horse/carriage, one-way. This could hardly be considered a manageable distance regarding Theo's supervision of his brother.

And Dr. Gachet, although a resident of Auvers-sur-Oise, had closed his practice in his hometown. Instead he traveled to Paris, several times a week. Considering available modes of transportation at that time this meant between that a roundtrip journey to and from Paris would require between 4 ½-6 hours in one day. This means that Dr. Gachet was physically absent from Auvers-sur-Oise for significant periods of time. This was certainly not an optimal situation regarding the supervision of a suicidal patient who'd just been released from an asylum.

Theo van Gogh was aware of all of these facts when he decided to place Vincent in Auver-sur-Oise after his release from St. Rémy. Giving Theo the benefit of doubt, perhaps these arrangements might have been acceptable for a person whose suicidal episodes (or severe melancholia) had occurred in the distant past of their patient history, but Vincent had attempted to commit suicide at least twice in the six months prior to his release from St. Rémy asylum:

- once by eating paint;
- once by drinking painting solvent while on a day excursion with a fellow painter/friend to his studio (the famous "Yellow House").

In fact, just prior to his release, Vincent writes (in his letters) that if he were to be released he would fear for his own safety (physically and psychologically).

Again,
(ACCORDING TO DAMIEN FALGOUST AT THE UNIVERSITY OF TEXAS SCHOOL OF LAW'S COURSE OUTLINE [FOR "CRIMINAL LAW"], 1996) some definitions:

SECTION G.   *"DEFENSES" TO INTENT*
  V.   *COMPLICITY*
        A.   *MODEL PENAL CODE (TEXAS FOLLOWS)*
      2.   *ACCOMPLICE*
           C.   *ONE WHO HAS A LEGAL DUTY TO PREVENT AN OFFENSE AND DOES NOT DO SO.*

Therefore, it could be argued that Theo van Gogh was either Recklessly or Negligently involved in Vincent van Gogh's suicide because he was Vincent's legal guardian (the person responsible for Vincent's discharge from St. Rémy) at the time when it occurred. Finally,
(ACCORDING TO DAMIEN FALGOUST AT THE UNIVERSITY OF TEXAS SCHOOL OF LAW'S COURSE OUTLINE [FOR "CRIMINAL LAW"], 1996) some definitions:

VI.   *HOMICIDE*
        B.   *GENERAL PRINCIPLES*
           1.   *MURDER VS. MANSLAUGHTER*
              b.   *MODERN PENAL CODES MAKE THE FOLLOWING DISTINCTIONS:*
                  1.   *MURDER: INTENTIONALLY OR KNOWINGLY CAUSING DEATH (SOME ADD RECKLESSLY WITH EXTREME INDIFFERENCE TO HUMAN LIFE)*
                  2.   *MANSLAUGHTER: RECKLESSLY CAUSING DEATH*
                  3.   *NEGLIGENT HOMICIDE: NEGLIGENTLY CAUSING DEATH.*
        D.   *VOLUNTARY MANSLAUGHTER*
           1.   *MURDER CAN BE MITIGATED TO MANSLAUGHTER IF THERE IS AN ADEQUATE PROVOCATION*
              3.)   *TEST FOR PROVOCATION*
                  c.   ***STATE V. RAGUSEO*** *– ACTOR OBSESSED WITH HIS PARKING SPACE GOES NUTS, STABS VICTIM WHO PARKED THERE.*
                    1.   *MAJORITY USES PURELY OBJECTIVE POINT OF VIEW IN EVALUATING THE REASONABLENESS OF THE ACTOR'S CONDUCT.*
                    2.   *DISSENT SAYS WE SHOULD DETERMINE IF THE ACTOR'S CONDUCT IS REASONABLE FOR A PERSON WITH THE ACTOR'S EMOTIONAL STATE.*

I don't believe, that it would be a huge stretch—in today's legal environment—(under the same circumstances surrounding Vincent van Gogh's death: his release from the asylum just one month prior, his history of suicidal tendencies, his release being secured under the pretense that his brother would provide appropriate care in the forms of his own supervision of his brother as well as professional/medical (psychological) which were not provided) that Theo van Gogh would be implicated in the painter's suicide.

NOTE OF INTEREST: A DEFENSE

There may have been, using today's standards, a legal defense regarding Theo van Gogh's state of mind at the time he secured Vincent's release from St. Rémy, if there could be proven that there was questionable lucidity as a result of contracting syphilis. It may be of interest that Theo van Gogh, in fact, died from complications from syphilis (including dementia with violence) just 6 months after the death of his brother, Vincent.

DID SOMEONE SAY MURDER?

CUTTING~SHOOTING~TRAVELLING

Yes, in fact, there was an accusation of murder made (the murder of Vincent van Gogh). Only contrary to what the police thought upon entering the scene (thinking that Vincent was dead), Vincent was only near-dead. The accused murderer: Paul Gauguin. This accusation is public record. The reference is, of course, the infamous "ear" removal at the Yellow House in Arles.

The police, upon receiving a tip, found Vincent van Gogh in bed—motionless, unresponsive and covered in blood. Naturally, they thought he was dead. In Arles, at that time, murder was not awfully uncommon.

When Paul Gauguin showed up at the scene they questioned him, "Why have you murdered your friend?" Paul Gauguin conveyed his story of what had occurred. Historians have found many inconsistencies with Gauguin's recollections. In today's legal climate this would also, I believe, draw closer scrutiny to the case.

There are some interesting facts: according to Paul Gauguin, on

December 24th, 1888 (a Monday—and Christmas Eve),
> he ate "dinner" (not to be confused with "supper" as dinner, typically, precluded supper with regard to time of day) and was attacked by Vincent van Gogh outside the café where Vincent menaced him with a razor but where Paul Gauguin thwarted the attack. He said that Vincent "ran off"and that he, Paul Gauguin, then went to a hotel (versus going to the house he shared with Vincent—the Yellow House) and slept until the next morning. The next day is:

December 25th, 1888 (a Tuesday—and Christmas). On
December 25th, 1888 (Christmas), according to Paul Gauguin,
> Gauguin goes to the Yellow House where police question him about "murder" but, eventually, release him. On that same day:

(December 25th, 1888/Christmas) Paul Gauguin is supposed to have
> sent a telegram to Theo van Gogh, (Vincent's brother/agent/legal guardian) who is living in Paris (which is approximately 463 miles from Arles—and by today's train—

would take a minimum of 4 ½ hours, one way), informing him of Vincent's cutting.

Some reports have Theo arriving in Arles, "late" on <u>Christmas Eve</u> <u>(December 24th, 1888).</u> Obviously, if this were true, this would be problematic to the authenticity of Gauguin's story.

The Arles newspaper published van Gogh's cut ear story on: <u>December 23rd,</u> 1888 (a <u>Sunday</u>). Again, problematic regarding verifiable fact because the dates/times/logistics just don't jive. Especially when you also consider this point of interest: prior to the ear incident, Paul Gauguin (in order to explain to the police the instability of Vincent) claimed that Vincent had previously attacked him in a café then slammed a newspaper clipping before him with the title:

"The Murderer Has Fled."

The assertion was that after Vincent had learned that Paul Gauguin was planning to leave Arles he was in a fit of agitation/despair/insanity, which both precluded and explained his act of "self-mutilation."

However, upon researching newspaper headlines for December 1888, the title, "The Murderer Has Fled," comes up for *The Morning Advertiser, London*—on <u>December 24th,</u> 1888 (a Monday—Christmas Eve— which was, according to Paul Gauguin, the day that Vincent had done the self-injury).

Upon reviewing this information, several questions come to mind. When *did* Vincent attack Paul Gauguin, throwing down the newspaper article (did it, in fact, occur *prior* to the ear incident)? If Paul Gauguin, as he states, was so exhausted after Vincent's attack outside the café (where Vincent brandished the razor) that he fell into a deep sleep (one that he did not wake from until later the next morning) when did he telegram Theo van Gogh about Vincent's ear incident?

It must have occurred *after* the police questioned him because he said did not know what Vincent had done until he came to the scene the following morning (when the police questioned him regarding the murder of Vincent van Gogh). For it to occur after the police questioning one could logically assume that it did not occur first thing in the morning. Nor, for that fact, early in the morning as

Paul Gauguin had been so exhausted. It might, then, be assumed that he could have risen later in the morning, therefore being questioned by the police, later still and so on.

If Paul Gauguin was not able to contact Theo by telegram until after he'd been questioned (on December 25th, 1888—Christmas day) there begs issues of logistics. Did trains run at all on Christmas day? How late did the telegraph operator work on Christmas day? If they did, what trains ran on Christmas day and at what times? Which did Theo take? How long was the train ride from Paris to Arles on Christmas day?

The questions regarding transportation and communication logistics are especially important because they directly relate to the actual death of Vincent van Gogh.

When Vincent was shot—in Auvers-sur-Oise (less than 22 miles from Paris, where Theo lived) Theo van Gogh was not notified of his brother's shooting (by telegram or other method) until the day after the shooting. Why?

Theo van Gogh was reported as receiving a hand-delivered note at his place of employment, Goupil, Paris, on the day after the shooting by Anton Hirschig. There seems to be some irregularities regarding Theo's actual whereabouts (and his wife's) at the time of the shooting. However the delivery of the note establishes his location at a set time and place—on the day *after*.

(Anton Hirschig was a Dutch artist who'd previously worked with Theo but who claimed he did not know his home address. The shooting, being on a Sunday, meant the Goupil, Paris, was closed. So Hirschig asserted that he had to wait until Monday morning in order to reach Theo at his workplace.
Anton Hirschig was also lodging at the Ravoux's, having arrived shortly after Vincent had.)

[Also note: that when Dr. Gatchet was informed of Vincent van Gogh's shooting—he did not inform Anton Hirschig of Theo van Gogh's address. This is suspicious as Dr. Gatchet had, with documentation, been to Theo's residence.]

Why wasn't a telegram sent to Theo after the shooting? Granted, there may not have been train service to Auvers-sur-Oise at that time but then why wasn't a telegram sent from the nearest station? Perhaps this, too, was not feasible. Then why wasn't a coach used to carry the message?

The reason given by Anton Hirschig (that he, Anton Hirschig, did not know Theo's home address) is not believable for several reasons. First, because Anton Hirschig had had business with Theo previously and it was not uncommon for Theo to entertain artists in his apartment. However, perhaps, Anton Hirschig had not been one of the artists he'd invited so, though not likely, he may not have known his home address. However, Dr. Gachet knew it and more importantly—Vincent knew it!

Vincent was, in fact, lucid. Though he was shot he still carried on conversations…he even smoked his pipe. Therefore it is impossible to believe that he "could not" convey information regarding his brother's residence. The other option is that he would not—but are we to believe that he would not tell his brother (his brother being a man lauded as his dearest friend) of his potentially fatal wound? This leaves two pressing questions: why did it take so long for Theo to arrive in Auvers-sur-Oise (in contrast with Theo's arrival in Arles) and could Vincent van Gogh's death have been prevented?

The question of time: had a telegram been sent (or a note delivered)—on that Sunday—it is possible that Vincent's life could have been saved…with *proper* medical attention.

Fact 1:

It took Theo longer to arrive at his brother's side after the "shooting" in Auvers-sur-Oise (factoring in slower transportation [horse/carriage] it still should have taken less than half the traveling time than it did for him (on Christmas day—) going more than twenty times as far) to arrive in Arles after the infamous "cutting."

Fact 2:

There is a condemning piece of evidence regarding Dr. Gatchet. He was *not* the only physician called in on Vincent van Gogh's case after the shooting. The innkeeper, Ravoux, in fact, sent for the local doctor, Dr. Masery. Dr. Masery, in fact, visited Vincent twice and discussed surgery with Dr. Gachet. Dr. Gatchet took control of the situation—acting as Vincent's primary/attending physician—and surgery was opted against. Surgery may have saved Vincent's life (there were soldiers who'd survived gut wounds when surgery to remove the bullets was performed quickly after such wounding. Of course many died, afterwards, from infection).

By not acting, *both* physicians—assured Vincent van Gogh's death. However, because Dr. Gachet assumed the role of his treating physician it is upon him the culpability falls. Dr. Gachet was the authority who signed Vincent van Gogh's death certificate.

It should also be noted that very little documentation was made by Dr. Gachet describing his patient's, Vincent van Gogh's, physical condition. For example, the gunshot. Was it through the clothing or did the clothing remain in tact? This may seem, to some, a small detail however it might lend a clearer assumption as to murder versus suicide. Many suicides, by gunshot to the abdomen, will—in fact—lift their clothing before shooting. It may sound bizarre, but it is the same principle as people who drown themselves—after removing their shoes. It is not always the case (with shoes or clothes) but would simply merit further investigation. There is a further issue and that is, if the clothing had been lifted (indicating more strongly a suicide) then there would be less complication with regard to successful abdominal surgery and the removal of a bullet (particularly the bullets available at that time). However, if the bullet traveled through the clothing (indicating more strongly the case for murder) then the likelihood of surgery being successful would be greatly diminished due to complications arising from infection as a direct result of the clothing particles being taken within the abdominal cavity.

Regardless, if the clothes were lifted then he had a greater chance of surviving as field surgeons were well capable of removing bullets from clean wounds, with relative success. If the clothes had been fired through then there should have been further criminal investigation. Either way, we would know far more than we do today had Dr. Gachet (having dismissed Dr. Masery) performed his duties competently.

WEAPONS! WEAPONS?

References are made regarding Vincent van Gogh's brandishing a razor. As a man and as an artist, it would be natural to have razors (not only to shave a face with but to cut canvas with). From a criminal investigation perspective, then, Vincent van Gogh's threatening of bodily harm (to others as well as himself) with a razor (or cutting device) fits his M.O. (modus operandi). By the nature of his previous action (self-mutilation by cutting—the ear) it would be more believable that his successful suicide would be a result of this weapon of choice. In fact, being totally unsupervised by his physician or brother and allowed to freely paint out in isolated parts of the countryside around Auvers-sur-Oise, it would be entirely believable that (as a suicidal person) he would use what was at his disposal: poisonous solvents, paints, and/or knives.

However, he used a gun. This complicates the issue, not severely, but to the extent that handguns were relatively expensive and not everyone had one. It is not to say that Vincent couldn't have secured a gun. People then, as some now, shared/gave/lent. If, for example, Vincent asked someone to borrow their gun—they might have given it to him.

Some say that Vincent got the gun from Ravoux, the innkeeper. It is possible, as he was his lodger. However, it must be remembered that Vincent had, in fact, only been lodging with Ravoux for a relatively short time and that, prior to him becoming a lodger, Ravoux had had no previous acquaintance with Vincent van Gogh. This calls into question, then, "Would a man lend a relative stranger something that expensive?" It's possible.

More disturbingly, some say that Dr. Gachet gave the gun to him. In light of being his attending physician— (as he asserts with the local physician after Vincent's shooting) this would, in fact, make him culpable for reckless/negligent homicide [please refer to legal definitions].

Regardless, the gun was never recovered (however his paints, materials, easel and painting were recovered from where he spent the day painting—and finishing—his last painting, which some speculate was "Wheat Field With Crows" claiming that it illustrates the painter's pending suicide).

There is only one outside mention made of Vincent van Gogh with a gun. It occurred in Paris—with his brother, Theo.

WHERE DID YOU SAY HE GOT SHOT?

GEOGRAPHY

Some say he shot himself in a "wheat" field. Some say "corn" field. I've been told that, at that time in European history, all crop fields were referred to as 'corn' fields (even if they were growing hops, wheat, barley, etc.). Regardless, most people who've been in or around crop-fields—during midsummer—know that there is nothing particularly startling about crows flying over crops.

In fact, it would be safe to say that if Vincent van Gogh had not painted crows over whatever kind of field he was in on July 19, 1890 then he may well have been trying to communicate some hidden message—an ulterior meaning—perhaps delving in the imaginative venue that Paul Gauguin had emphasized in his painting while in the Midi.

However, the fact that he paints crows at that time in the growing season merely illustrates that he is painting what, literally, lay before his eyes. This corresponds to his writings about painting— the return to the beauty of more concrete| true representation—after his institutionalization.

I.   WOULDN'T SOMEONE HAVE HEARD A GUNSHOT?

Some think it would be unlikely that the sound of a gunshot would be missed by the farmers in the fields. However, it would be unlikely to *have* farmers in either wheat or cornfields on July 29, 1890. The crops would have been simply growing at that time. In the off-chance that someone *had* heard a gunshot they would not have had any bearing as to where it came from and, most likely, would have simply dismissed it and carried on with their work.

II.   BLOOD TRAIL, HOWEVER: IT'S AS SIMPLE AS THIS.

There was one. Did the blood trail lead a person/people to where he'd last been painting (as his materials were recovered)? If so, where was the gun? If not, how did they find the art supplies?

III. DID HE CONFESS?

Did Vincent tell them where to find his art supplies/easel? Would he not, then, tell where he'd shot himself? Was it the same location as where he'd been painting or did he leave his art supplies unattended? This last question is important because Vincent's MO would not support the idea that he would abandon what he valued: his (literally expensive) materials. It would be totally uncharacteristic for him to leave them where they could be lost, destroyed and/or stolen. If there was one dominant characteristic in Vincent van Gogh (as it pervades all of his published volumes of writing) it was the value he placed upon paints/paint supplies. It would be uncharacteristic, even in suicide, for him to disregard them in such a manner therefore, logically, it could be assumed that he kept them in his possession— and shot himself. So where's the gun?

WHERE DID YOU SAY HE GOT SHOT?

ANATOMY

There are many claims as to where, anatomically, Vincent van Gogh was shot:

- the heart
- the genitals
- the, literal, stomach
- the intestines/liver

Based on research the first two would be unlikely, as the rate of death would not fit the timeframe reported for Vincent van Gogh's death. Regarding length of time to die after sustaining the injury, the third and fourth options are both possible. There was one report that at the funeral, when the casket is being lifted onto the cart, a foul greenish substance leaked out of the corner of the casket. If this was true, then it would support the latter anatomical location: the intestines/liver.

SUSPECTS

Suspect #1
Vincent van Gogh: Suicide—
> Case: pre-existing suicide attempts leading to admission to both hospital (psychiatric) and asylum.

Suspect #2
Theo van Gogh: Negligent/Reckless Homicide/Manslaughter—
> Case: knowingly put victim at risk of harm (based on pre-existing psychiatric condition) with means to do harm (paints/knives/unattended and isolated excursions).

Suspect #3
Dr. Paul Gatchet: Malpractice—
> Case: knowingly put victim at risk of harm (based on pre-existing psychiatric condition) with means to do harm (paints/knives/unattended and isolated excursions) and possibly provided the victim with the gun that killed him.

POSSIBLE MOTIVES

Vincent van Gogh:
> Insanity—(possibly due to chronic exposure to the hazardous materials of his trade and drug use as well as having contracted syphilis).

Theo van Gogh:
> Financial—(to be released from financially supporting his brother in light of his recent marriage to Jo Bonger [note: it is this financial dependence that has been used to support the assertion that Vincent van Gogh killed himself because of resulting guilt over the said "dependence"] and immediately after Vincent van Gogh's death he facilitated the transfer of his mother's and sister's legal claims to Vincent van Gogh's work—indicating he placed some value on the works),
>
> Insanity—(possibly due to drug use and/or having contracted syphilis).

Dr. Gatchet:
> Financial—(he accumulated a significant body of Vincent van Gogh's work {that, after his death, eventually amounted to a relative fortune} as well as producing (forgeries/practice) copies of Vincent's work which enabled him to insert himself into Art community). Note of interest: some of Dr. Gachet's 'copies' have been sold as authentic.

SUCCESS OR NOT SUCCESS: THAT IS THE QUESTION.

It has become part of the legend that Vincent van Gogh was a penniless artist who never sold paintings and who lived reclusively. There is a mythos about such artists (in all fields) that propels them into iconoclastic history—and mystery.

However, it would be too simplistic to apply these generalities to Vincent van Gogh's body of work, while he was living. In fact, although he sold minimal numbers of paintings (primarily to family) he did exchange them in trade for things such as painting supplies, rent, etc.

The barter system is an economic model. It is one that Vincent van Gogh participated in. He valued his works and exchanged, based on assessed value, for things he needed. And, it should be noted, that what he valued his work at was not "cheap" with regard to the standards of the time.

It has been said that when Vincent van Gogh died he was relatively unknown. Certainly he was no Renoir. However, he'd had an article written about him in an art journal and he'd been asked to display his work beside other (more well-known) Impressionists (for example: Henri-de Toulouse Lautrec).

To all outward appearances, Vincent van Gogh was on an upward arc. He was becoming accepted in the art community (refer to: Claude-Emile Schuffenecker). So why, after all those years of work and actively trying to get his work sold (when you read his entire body of letters is it clearly evident that selling was Vincent van Gogh's primary goal), would he take his own life?

Perhaps too sell...more? Could not that also be the motive for murder?

PHYSICAL EVIDENCE:

NO GUN, NO CLOTHES, NO…BUT WAIT

There is one final thought I would like to leave you with. The letters. There are more than 1,200 pages of letters written by Vincent van Gogh, which have been translated and published by Jo van Gogh-Bonger (she and Theo began promoting Vincent's work within days after his death). Yet, there are very few surviving letters from Theo van Gogh. This, if nothing else, should resound strangely.

If one best judges another by their actions, then by the fact that Vincent van Gogh wrote voluminously and consistently it should make evident that he placed a great deal of value upon writing/correspondence.

More germane to the issue is that when one reads Vincent van Gogh's letters it is striking how systematically he makes specific references to certain passages of the letters he has received from the writer (whether it is from his brother, mother, friends, or compatriots). This indicates that he practiced analyzing the letters, then carefully re-iterated (using exact phrasings from the writer's letter) in order to produce his response.

With regard to his letters to his brother, Theo, there is much evidence to support the fact that Vincent kept Theo's correspondences (he makes specific, verbatim, references to letters he'd received from his brother's several correspondences prior). What happened to all of those letters, all of Theo's letters?

CONCLUSION

Neither I, nor you—my Dear Reader—will ever know what happened to Vincent van Gogh. That is the point. His life, and death, has entered into the realm of Mythos, which is why I've written this story and why I've given you these tidbits of "fact." But Fact does not a Truth make:

> *"All things are subject to interpretation. Whichever interpretation prevails at a given time is a function of power and not truth."* FRIEDRICH NIETZSCHE

I am, after all, simply a writer
and Everyone knows that Writers
are the most notorious liars!

The Murder of Vincent van Gogh:
Bibliography/References—

TEXTS
1) Bullfinch Press Book. <u>The Complete Letters of Vincent Van Gogh (volumes I, II, and III)</u>. Little, Brown and Company, New York. 2000

2) Bunyan, John; Schmidt, Gary D.; and Moser, Barry. <u>Pilgrim's Progress: A Retelling.</u> (Hardcover) Wm B. Eerdmans Publishing Co. September, 1994

3) Cutts, Josephine; and Smith, James. <u>Van Gogh</u>. Parragon Publishing, UK. 2001

4) Downie, David. <u>Paris, Paris: Journey Into the City of Light.</u> David Downie. 2005

5) Fell, Darek. <u>Van Gogh's Women: His Love Affairs and Journey Into Madness</u>. Da Capo Press. November 2, 2004

6) Huyghe, René. <u>Van Gogh</u>. Crown Publishers, Inc., New York. 1977

7) Lubin, Albert J. <u>Stranger on the Earth: A Psychological Biograghy of Vincent van Gogh.</u> Da Capo Press, 1996

8) Lucas, Eileen. <u>Vincent van Gogh</u>. First Book; Franklin Watts; Eileen Lucas, New York. 1991

9) Ozanne, Marie-Angelique; and de Jade, Frederique. <u>Theo: The Other van Gogh</u>. Abram, Harry N Inc. April 2004

10) Rewald, John. <u>Post-Impressionism From Van Gogh to Gauguin</u>. The Museum of Modern Art, New York. 1962

11) Sweetman, David. <u>Van Gogh: His Life and His Art</u>. Crown Publishers, New York. 1990

12) Stolwikj, Chris; and Veenenbos, Han. <u>The Account Book of Theo van Gogh and Jo van Gogh-Bonger.</u> Publisher: John Rule. ISBN 90 74310 826

13) Van Gogh, Theo; van Gogh-Bonger, Jo; and Jansen, Leo. <u>Brief Happiness: The Correspondence of Theo van Gogh and Jo Bonger.</u> B.V. Waanders Vitgeverj. 2000.

14) Wallace, Robert; and the Editors of Time-Life Books. <u>The World of Van Gogh 1853-1890</u>. Time Inc, New York. 1969

WEB
1) www.casebook.org/press_reports/morning_advertiser/188 8122…(Search: "The Murderer Has Fled…")
2) www.soulcast.com/post/shot/101629/Gogh,-Vincent-Willem-van-(1853-1890)
3) www.writing-world.com (Search: "difference between murder and suicide")
4) http://au.answers.yahoo.com (Search: "how long would someone survive after getting shot in these areas")
5) www.littlegun.be (Search: handguns of (or available in) 1890)
6) www.law.cornell.edu (Search: "Murder" by legal definition—including "Negligent Homicide" and "Manslaughter")
7) http://archiver.rootsweb.com/th/read/BOER-WAR/2001-04/0986671531 (Search: "Boer War" and "Cor van Gogh")
8) www.wikipedia.org (Search: "Boer War," "Second Boer War," "King William III or the Netherlands," "Vincent van Gogh," "Vincent van Gogh Chronology")
9) www.en.wikipedia.org (Search: "Seppuku," "Vincent van Gogh")
10) www.vggallery.com (Search: Online Forum and "gun" and "firearm" and "Dr. Gachet." Search: "Jo Bonger's memoirs" Search: "Memoirs of Vincent van Gogh's Stay in Auverys-sur-Oise by Adeline Ravoux".)
11) www.vangohgalley.com (Search: "David Brooks" and "Vincent van Gogh")
12) www.iisg.nl/archives/en/files/m/10909020full.php (Search: "Louise Michel Papers")
13) www.skeptics.com (Search: "Letter 653: Auvers-Sur-Oise, June 16, 1980)
14) www.webexhibit.org (Search: "Anton Hirschig")
15) www.bloodfinderofnh.com (Search: "After The Shot, Blood In Motion: A Forensic Guide to Blood Tracking")
16) http://esynopsis.uchc.edu (Search: "Gun Shot Wound to Stomach")
17) www.igougo.com (Search: "Auvers_sur-Oise" and "House of van Gogh")

18) www.amjforensicmedicine.com (Search: "Prolonged Activity After an Ultimately Fatal Gunshot Wound to the Heart: Case Report" and "A Suicide Diguised as a Homicide: Return to Thor Bridge")

19) http://artwell.com (Search: Was Van Gogh's Aural Mutilation Premeditated?")

20) www.unitedathletes.com (Search: "Interview with Roberto Galan: The Life of a matador." Published: March 20, 2006")

21) www.ajp.psychiatryonline.org (Search: "The Illness of Vincent van Gogh")

22) http://krant.telegrauf.nl (Search: "Cornelius van Gogh")

23) www.absinthebuyersguide.com (Search: Vincent van Gogh")

24) www.paintingdrawing.suite101.com (Search: "Vincent van Gogh-Starry Night")

25) www.thehollandring.com (Search: "Vincent van Gogh")

26) www.artquotes.net (Search: "Vincent van Gogh")

27) www.nndb.com (Search: "Vincent van Gogh")

28) www.cronaca.com (Search: "Van Gogh had a Son?")

29) www.britannica.com (Search: Vincent van Gogh: The Productive Decade")

30) www.pep-web.org (Search: "The Inner World of Paul Gauguin")

31) www.abcgallery.com (Search: "Paul Gauguin Biography")

32) www.diplomatic.gouv.fr (Search: "Gauguin's Tahiti Years at the Grand Palais")

33) www.iht.com (Search: "Books: Brief Happiness— Correspondence of Theo van Gogh and Jo Bonger")

34) www.webexhibits.org (Search: "Memoir of Johanna Gesina van Gogh-Bonger")

35) www.dalehobson.org (Search: "Notes for Provencal Light")

36) http://blogs.princeton.edu (Search: "Paul Gauguin: The Noble Savage)

NEWSPAPER
1) The New York Times, published: December 14, 1914, "Major Gen. Brabant Dies. Boer War Hero Was Knighted in 1900—In 76th Year."
2) http://query.nytimes.com (Search: "Vincent Obsessed" published: August 12, 1990," "Gored" published: October 15, 1995)
3) The Art Newspaper, "Cezanne joins Van Gogh for close scrutiny." No. 90, March 1999, pages 10-12 (Search: "Wheat Field" versus "Corn Field")

JOURNALS/ARTICLES
1) International Journal of Legal Medicine, Volume 106/ Number 2/(online issue), March, 1993. (Search: "1899 Hague Declaration" and "Gunshot Wounds, Wound Ballistics, Bullet Fragmentation)
2) Peltier, Philippe. "Gauguin and Tahiti." Art Tribal, Summer/Autumn 2003.

www.ingramcontent.com/pod-product-compliance
Lightning Source LLC
Chambersburg PA
CBHW030526020726
47494CB00004B/1244